WAY, way back IN THE WILDEST OF WILD WESTS, ONE COWBOY left his mark behind.

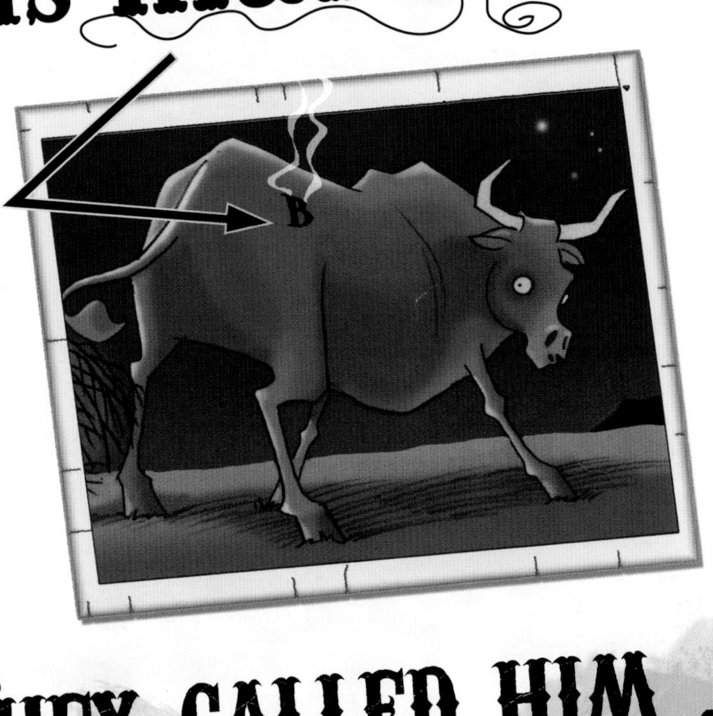
B

THEY CALLED HIM . . .

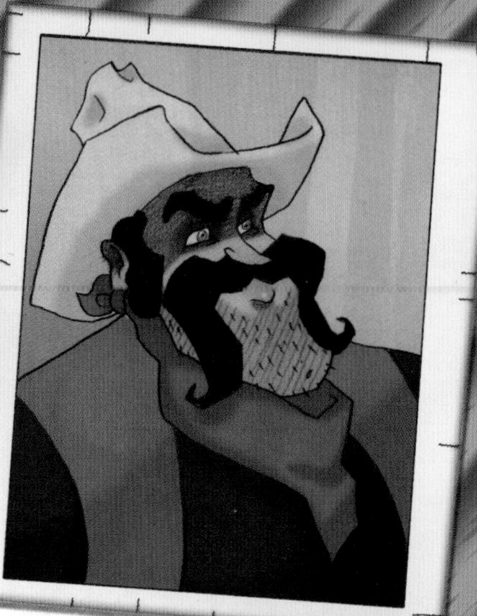

**GRAPHIC SPIN IS PUBLISHED BY STONE ARCH BOOKS**
A Capstone Imprint
151 Good Counsel Drive, P.O. Box 669
Mankato, Minnesota 56002
www.capstonepub.com



Library of Congress Cataloging-in-Publication Data

Tulien, Sean.
Pecos Bill, colossal cowboy : the graphic novel / retold by Sean Tulien ; illustrated by Lisa K. Weber.
p. cm. -- (Graphic spin)
ISBN 978-1-4342-1896-4 (library binding) -- ISBN 978-1-4342-2267-1 (pbk.)
1. Pecos Bill (Legendary character)--Legends. 2. Graphic novels. [1. Graphic novels. 2. Pecos Bill (Legendary character)--Legends. 3. Folklore--United States. 4. Tall tales.] I. Weber, Lisa K., ill. II. Title.
PZ7.7.T85Pe 2010
741.5'973--dc22

2009029100

Summary: Tossed from a wagon and raised by coyotes, Pecos Bill had a strange childhood to say the least. As he grows up, this Texas-sized cowboy wrestles with wolves, grapples with a wild mare, and rides a mountain lion without even breaking a sweat! Pecos Bill is able to tame the Wild West with ease, but soon he faces an even bigger challenge, a rampaging cyclone the likes of which no one has ever seen! Pecos Bill must try to rein in this wild storm, or it will lay waste to the great American frontier.

Printed in the United States of America in Stevens Point, Wisconsin.
092009
005619WZS10

**DESIGNER: KAY FRASER**
**EDITOR: DONALD LEMKE**
**ART DIRECTORS: KAY FRASER AND BOB LENTZ**

# PECOS BILL

retold by Sean Tulien
illustrated by Lisa Weber

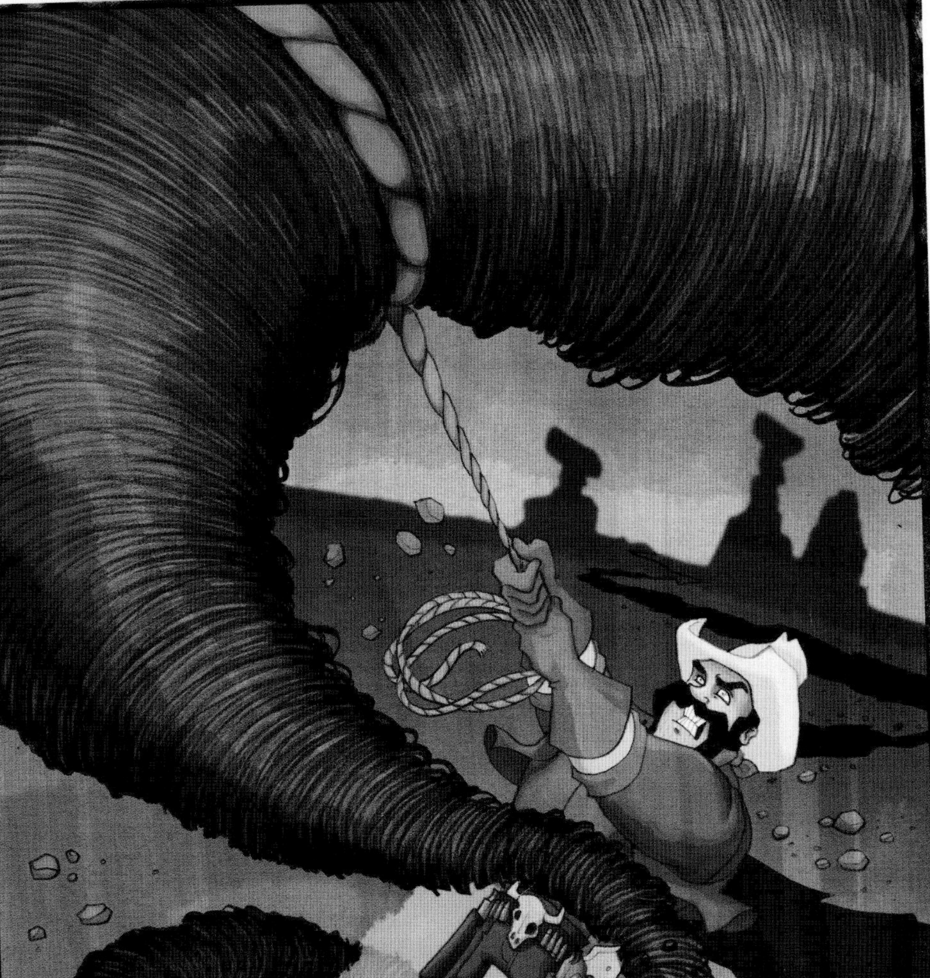

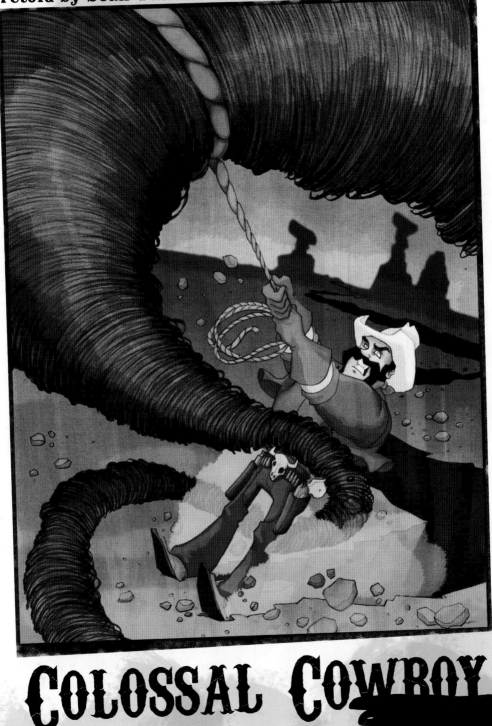

# COLOSSAL CO[redacted]

STONE ARCH BOOKS [redacted]
a capstone imprint

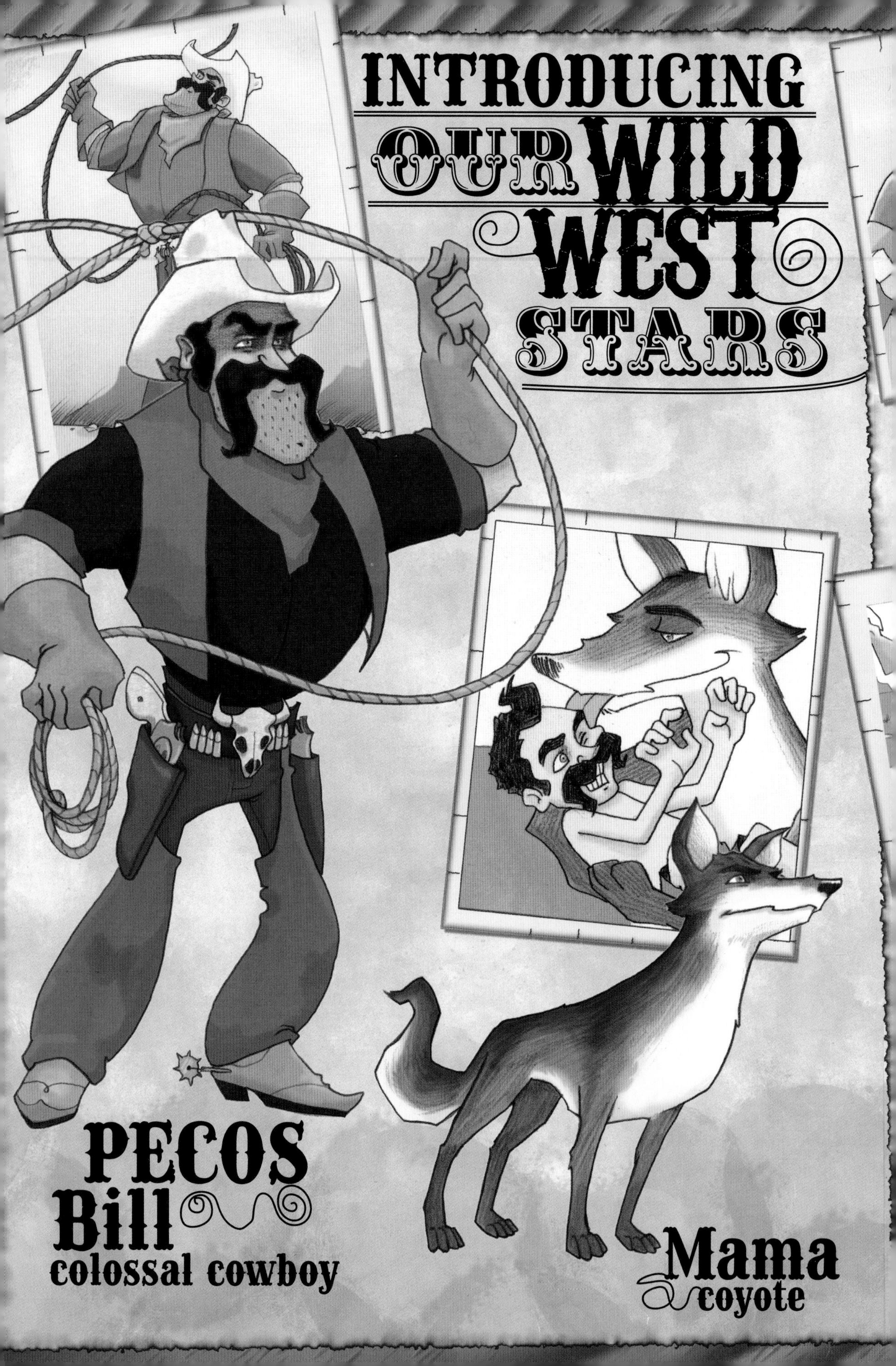
INTRODUCING
OUR WILD WEST STARS
PECOS Bill
colossal cowboy
Mama
coyote

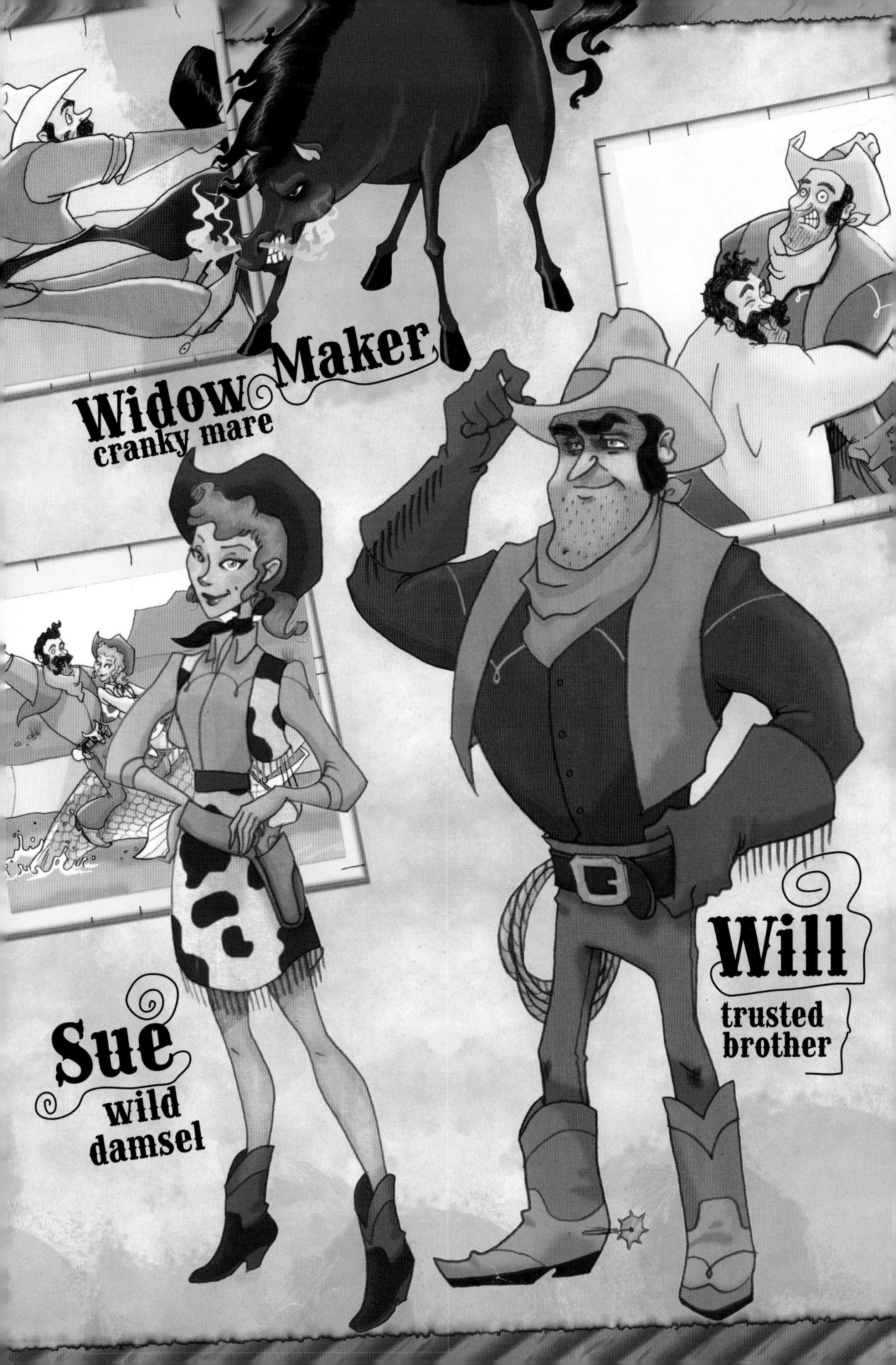
Widow Maker
cranky mare
Sue
wild damsel
Will
trusted brother

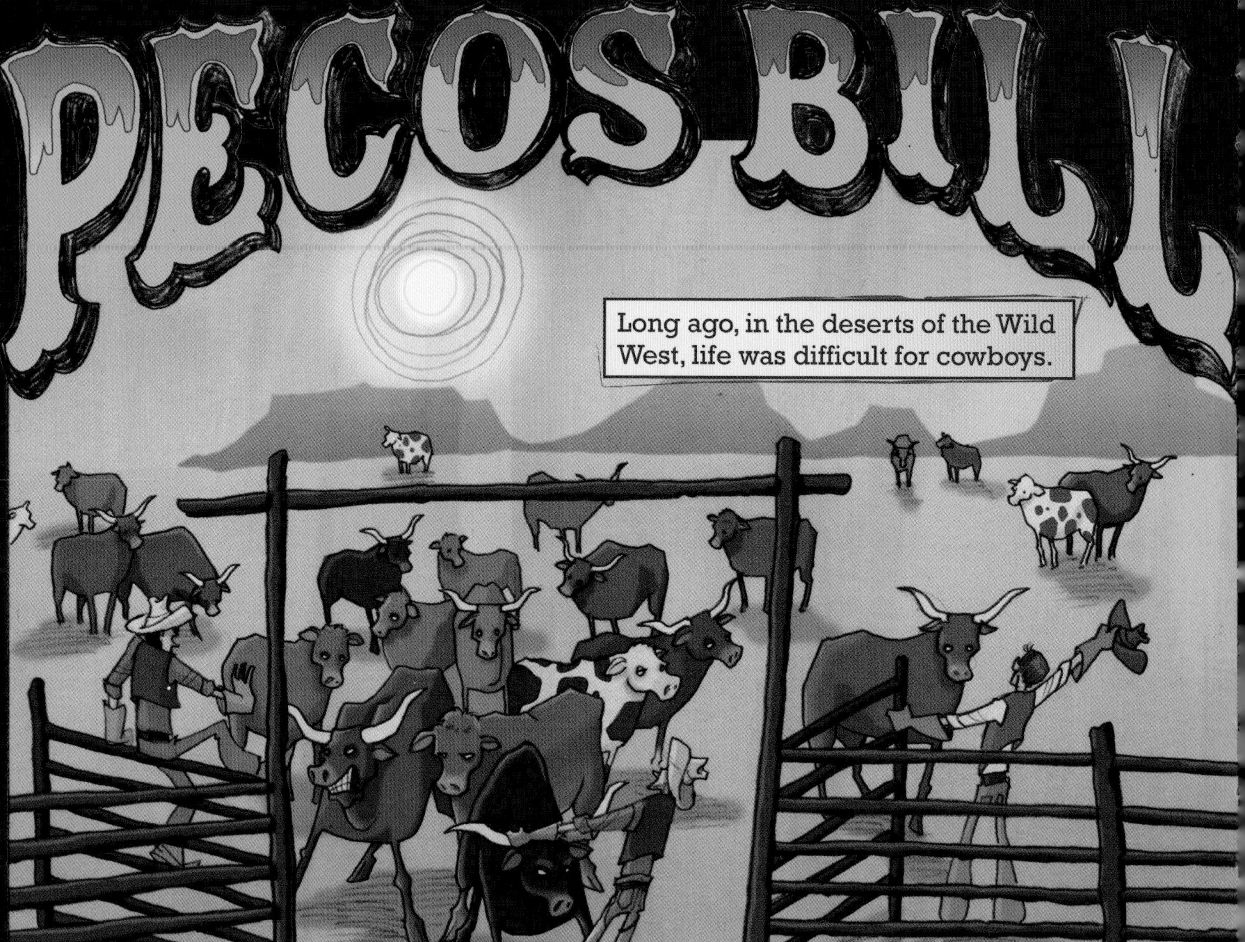
PECOS BILL
Long ago, in the deserts of the Wild West, life was difficult for cowboys.

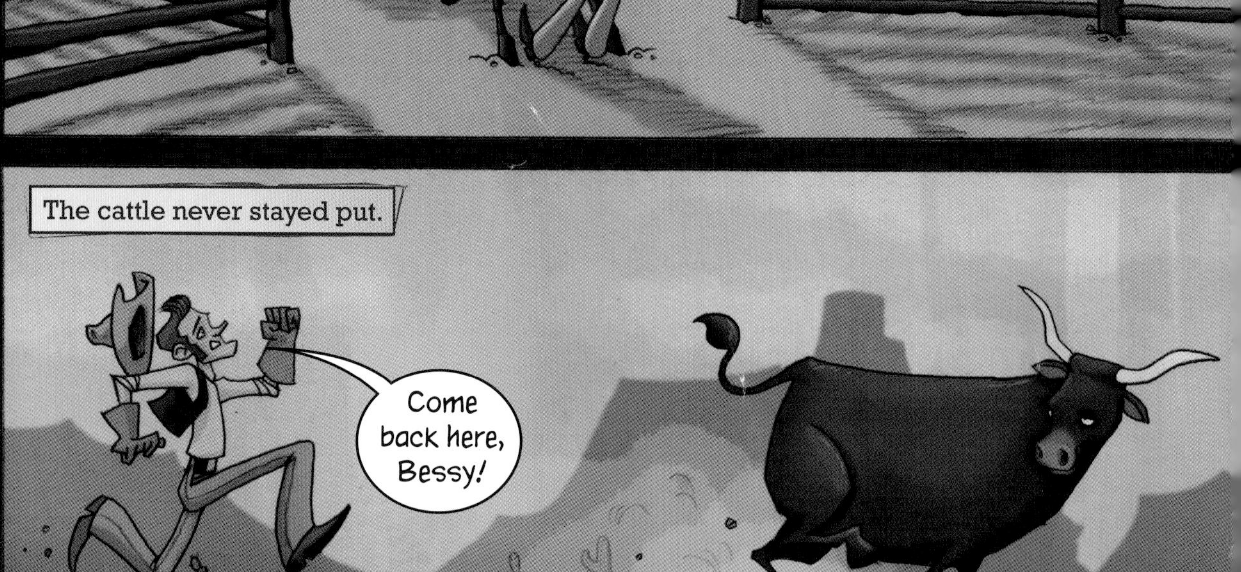
The cattle never stayed put.
Come back here, Bessy!

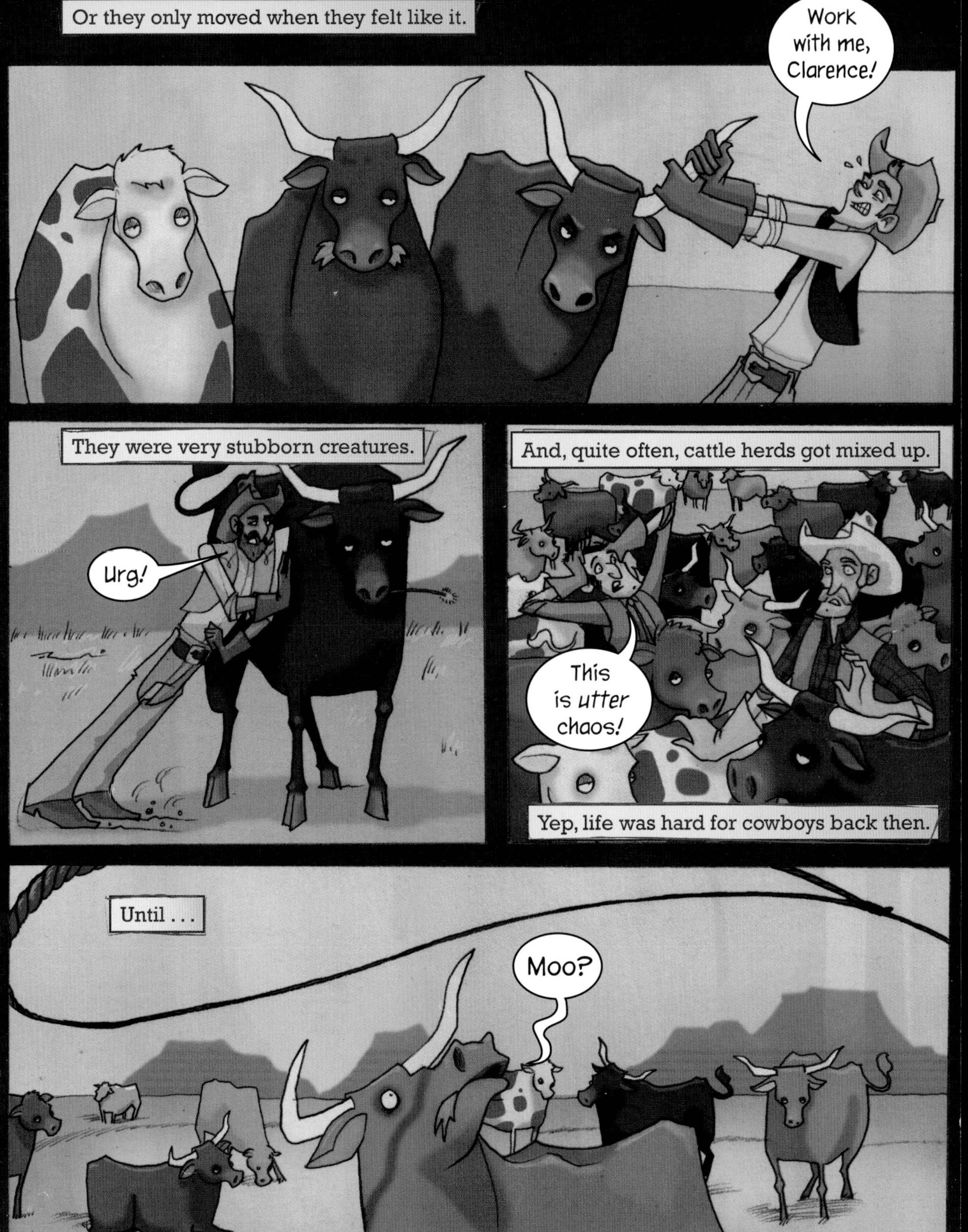
Or they only moved when they felt like it.
Work with me, Clarence!
They were very stubborn creatures.
Urg!
And, quite often, cattle herds got mixed up.
This is *utter* chaos!
Yep, life was hard for cowboys back then.
Until . . .
Moo?

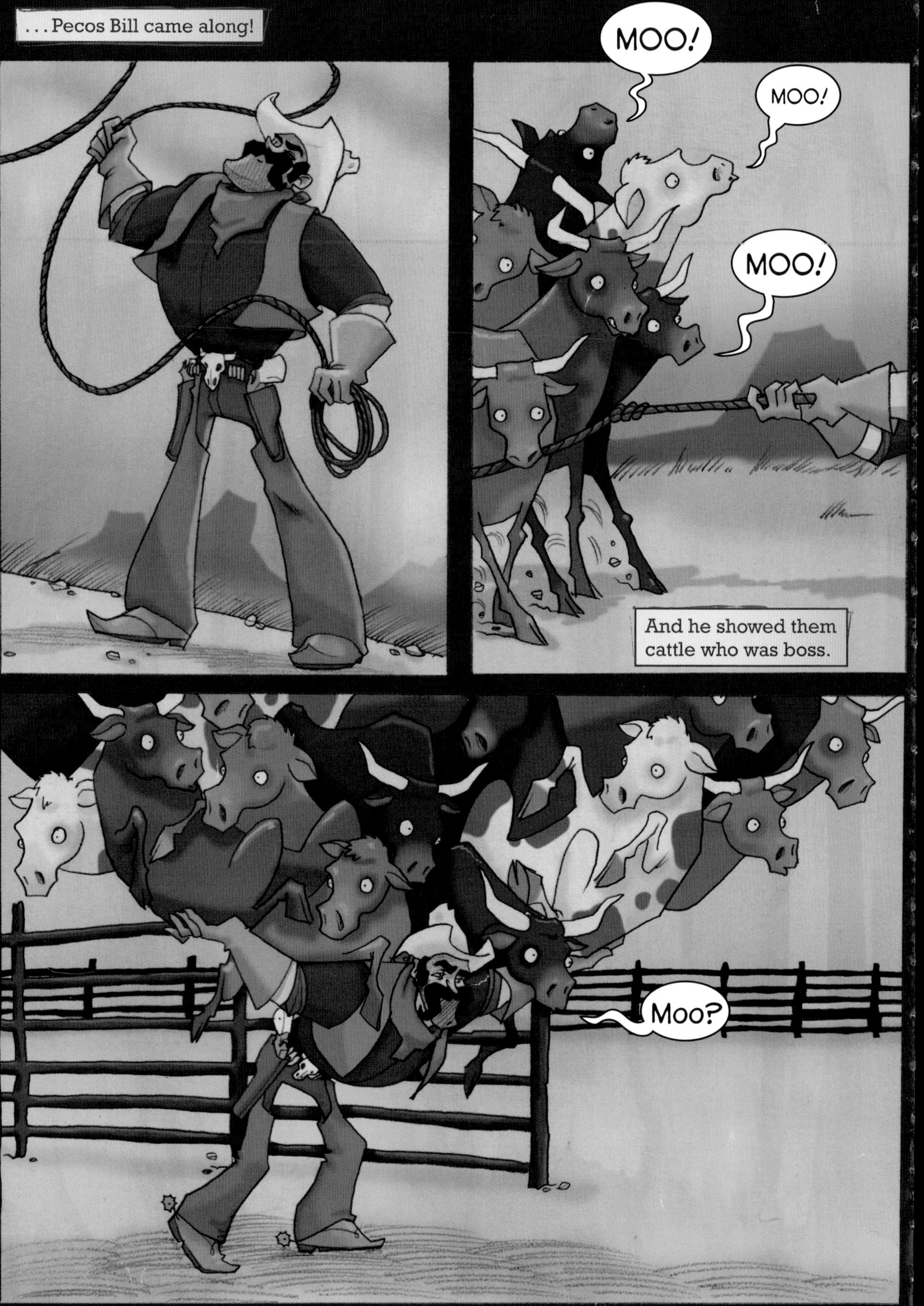

. . . Pecos Bill came along!
MOO!
MOO!
MOO!
And he showed them cattle who was boss.
Moo?

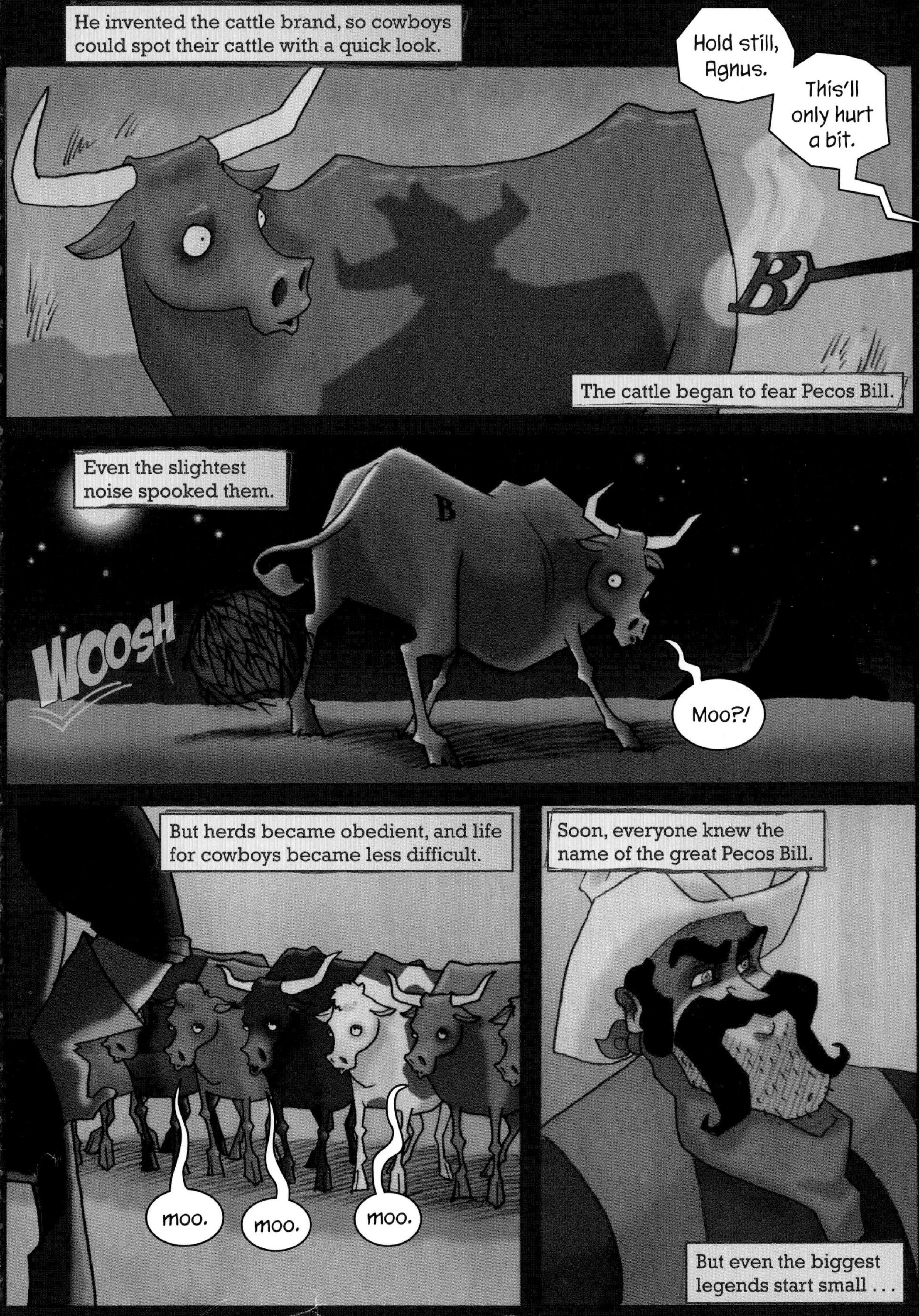
He invented the cattle brand, so cowboys could spot their cattle with a quick look.
Hold still, Agnus.
This'll only hurt a bit.
B
The cattle began to fear Pecos Bill.
Even the slightest noise spooked them.
B
WOOSH
Moo?!
But herds became obedient, and life for cowboys became less difficult.
moo.
moo.
moo.
Soon, everyone knew the name of the great Pecos Bill.
But even the biggest legends start small . . .

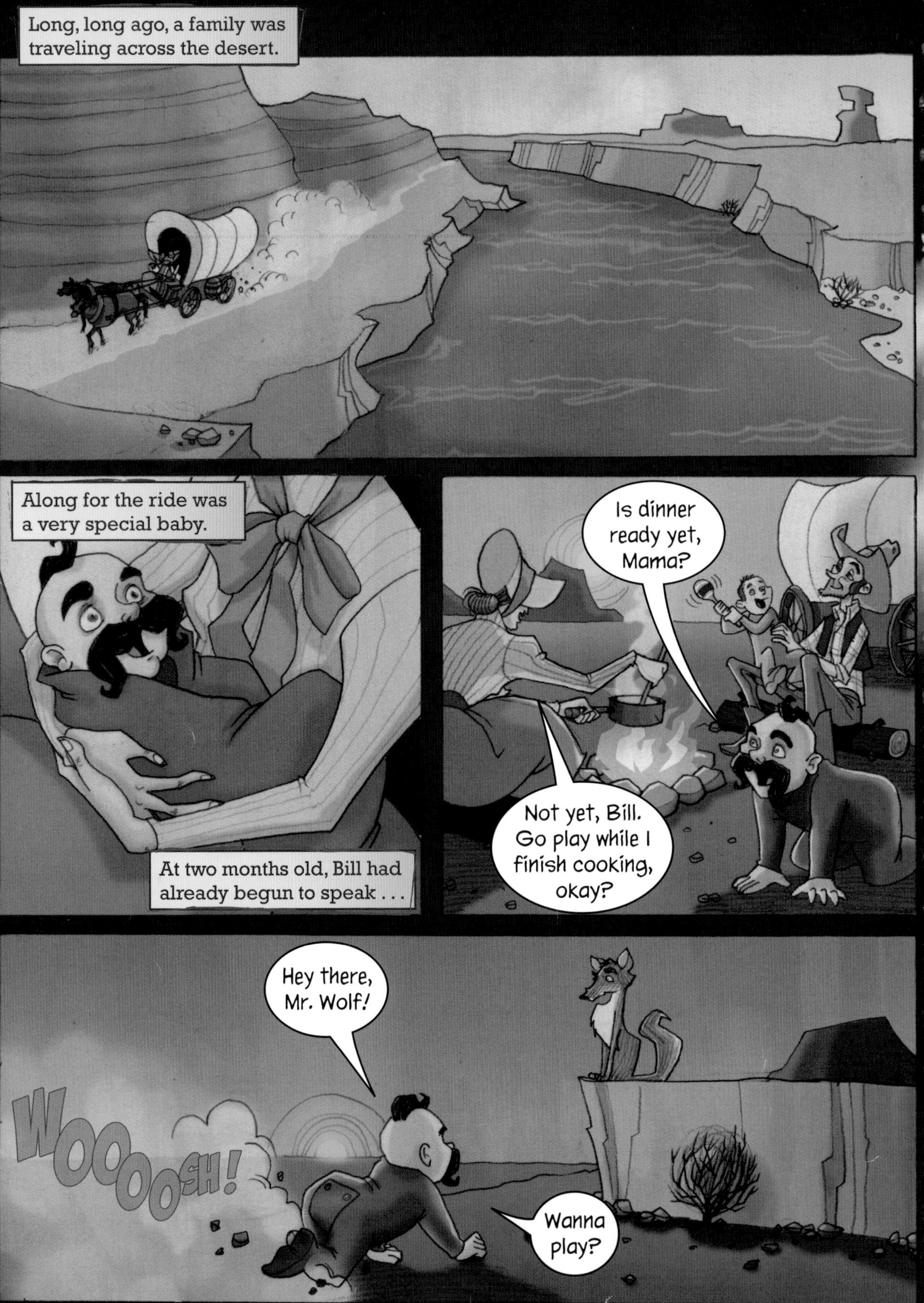
Long, long ago, a family was traveling across the desert.
Along for the ride was a very special baby.
At two months old, Bill had already begun to speak . . .
Is dinner ready yet, Mama?
Not yet, Bill. Go play while I finish cooking, okay?
Hey there, Mr. Wolf!
WOOOOOSH!
Wanna play?

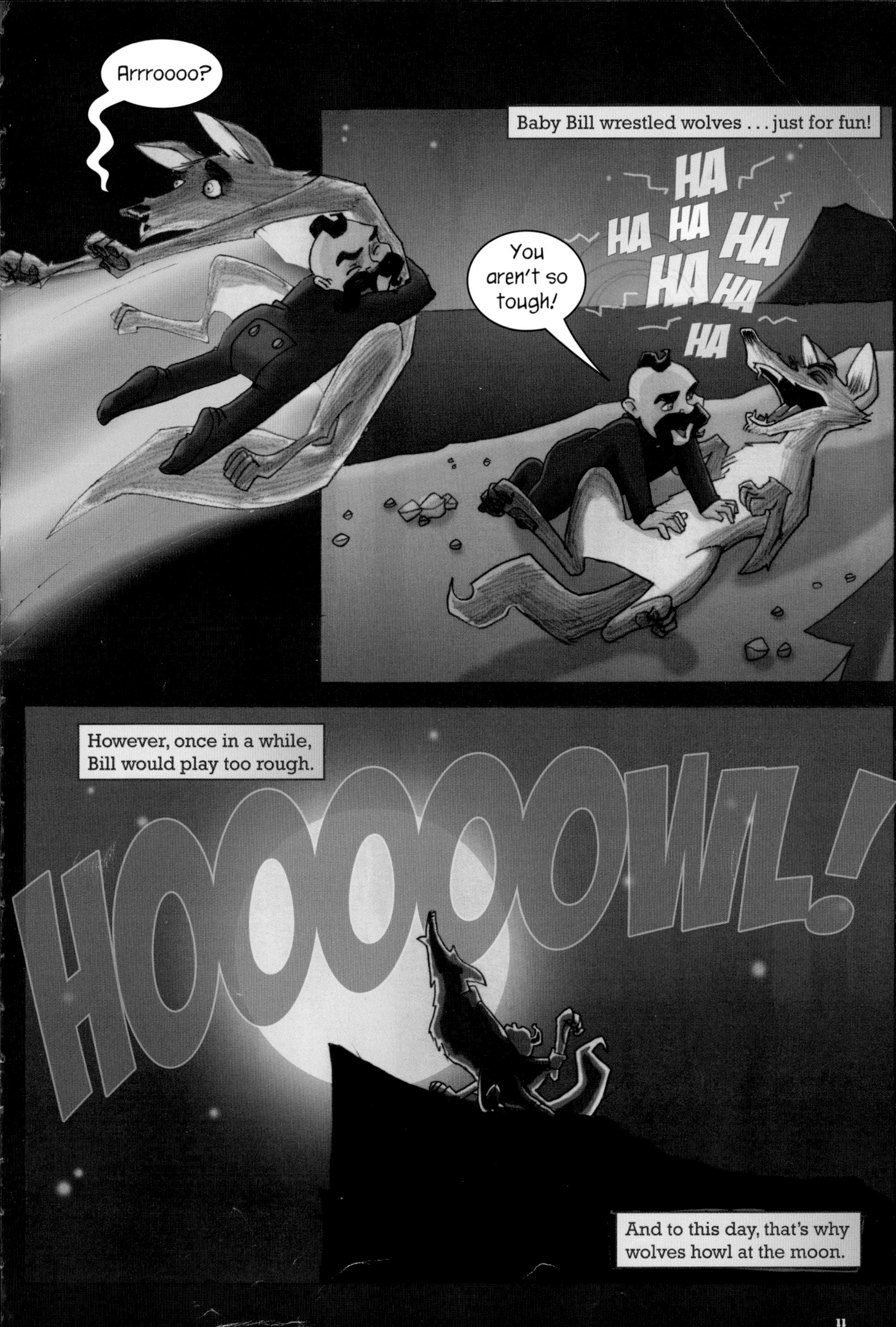

Arrroooo?
Baby Bill wrestled wolves . . . just for fun!
HA HA HA HA HA HA HA
You aren't so tough!
However, once in a while, Bill would play too rough.
HOOOOOWL!
And to this day, that's why wolves howl at the moon.

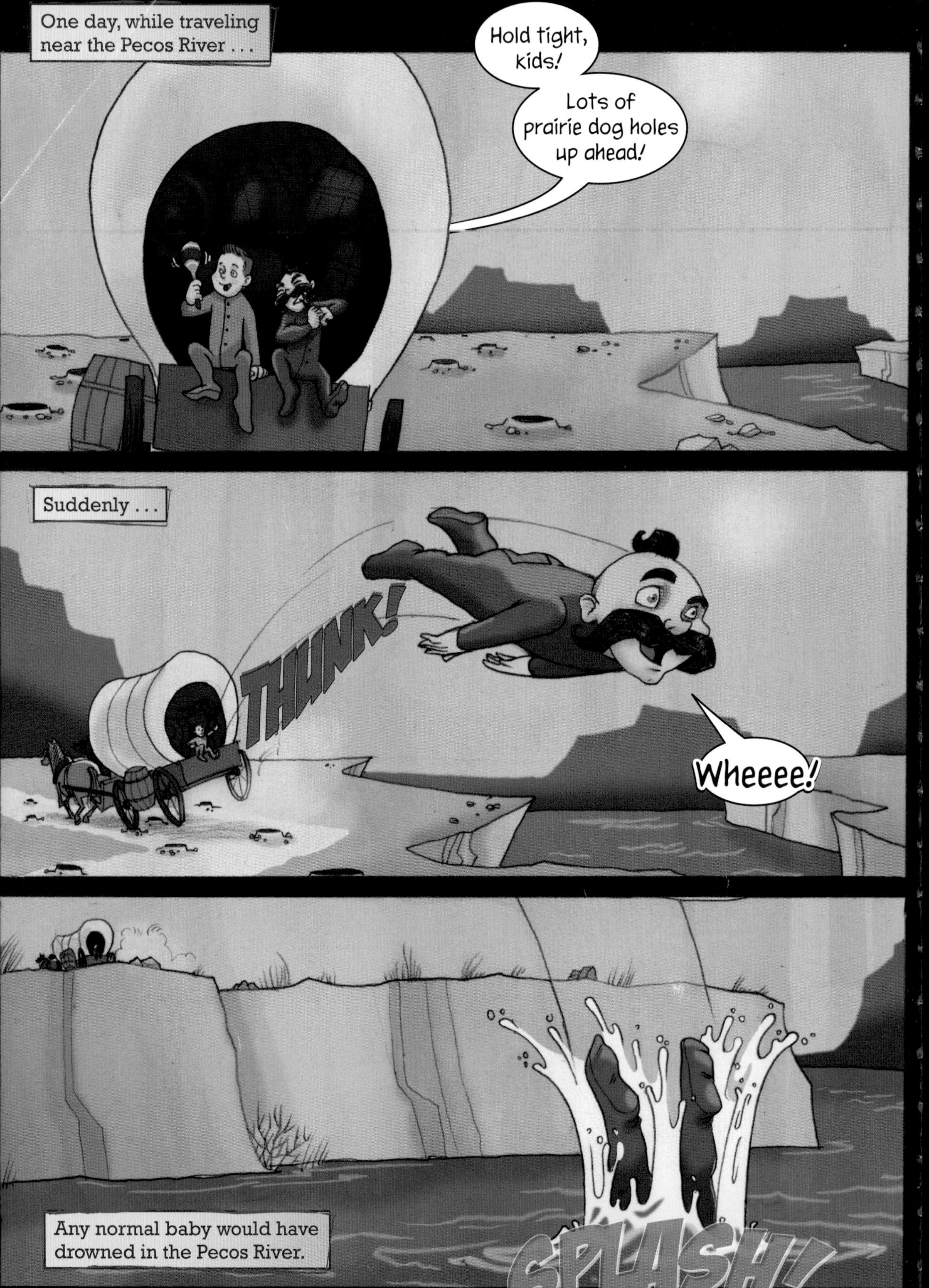

One day, while traveling near the Pecos River . . .
Hold tight, kids!
Lots of prairie dog holes up ahead!
Suddenly . . .
THUNK!
Wheeee!
Any normal baby would have drowned in the Pecos River.
SPLASH!

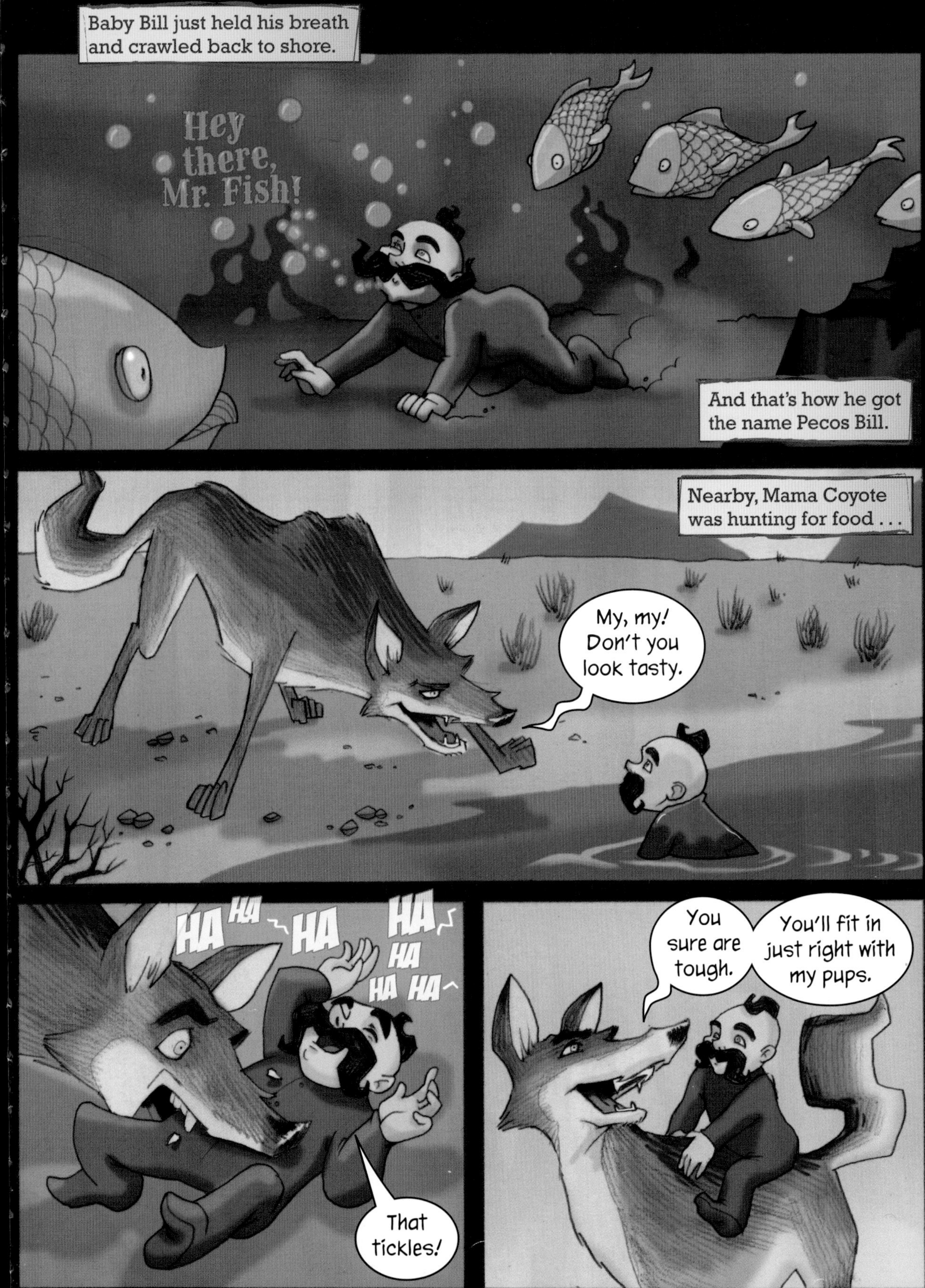

Baby Bill just held his breath and crawled back to shore.
Hey there, Mr. Fish!
And that's how he got the name Pecos Bill.
Nearby, Mama Coyote was hunting for food . . .
My, my! Don't you look tasty.
HA HA HA HA HA HA HA
That tickles!
You sure are tough.
You'll fit in just right with my pups.

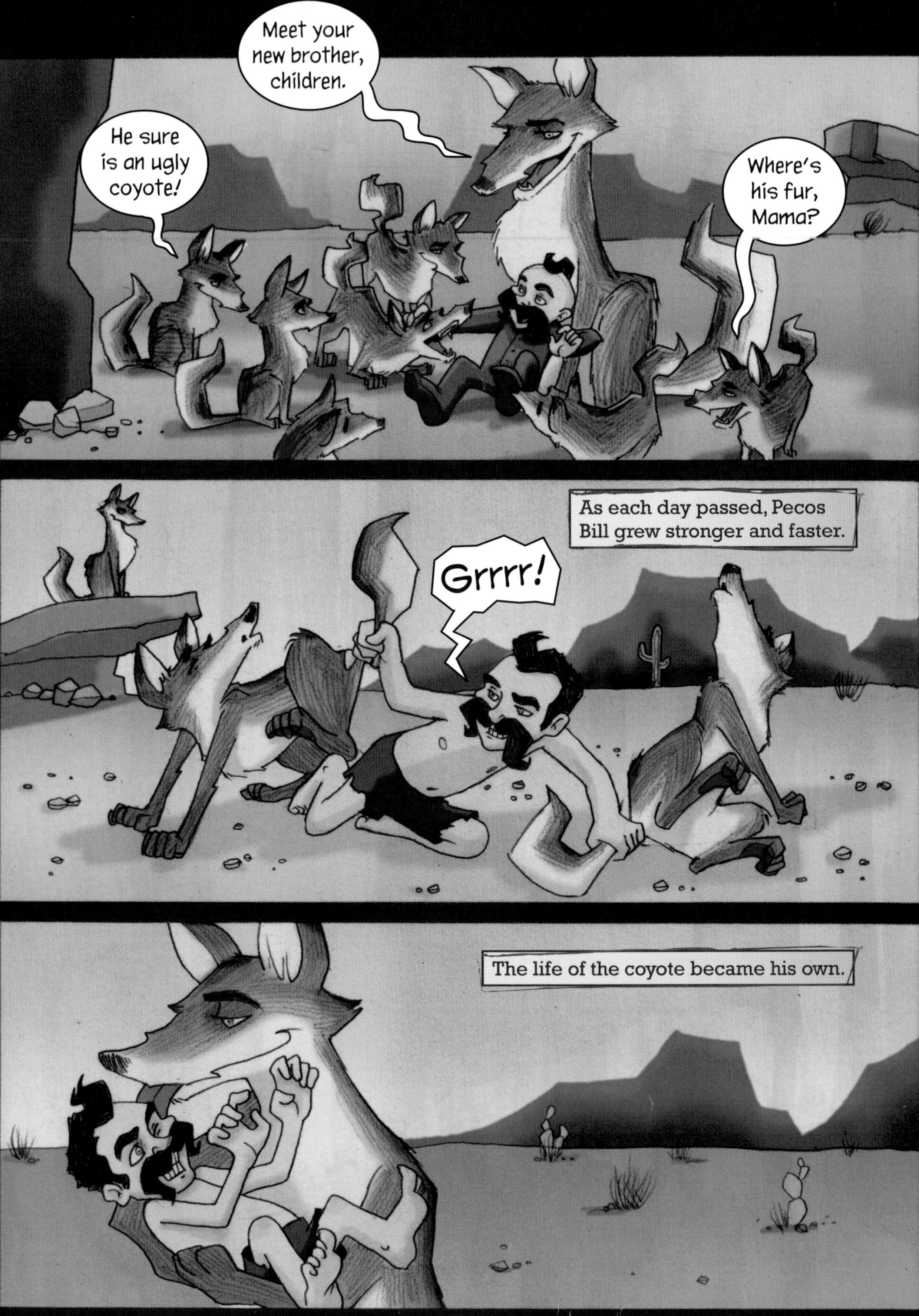
Meet your new brother, children.
He sure is an ugly coyote!
Where's his fur, Mama?
As each day passed, Pecos Bill grew stronger and faster.
Grrrr!
The life of the coyote became his own.

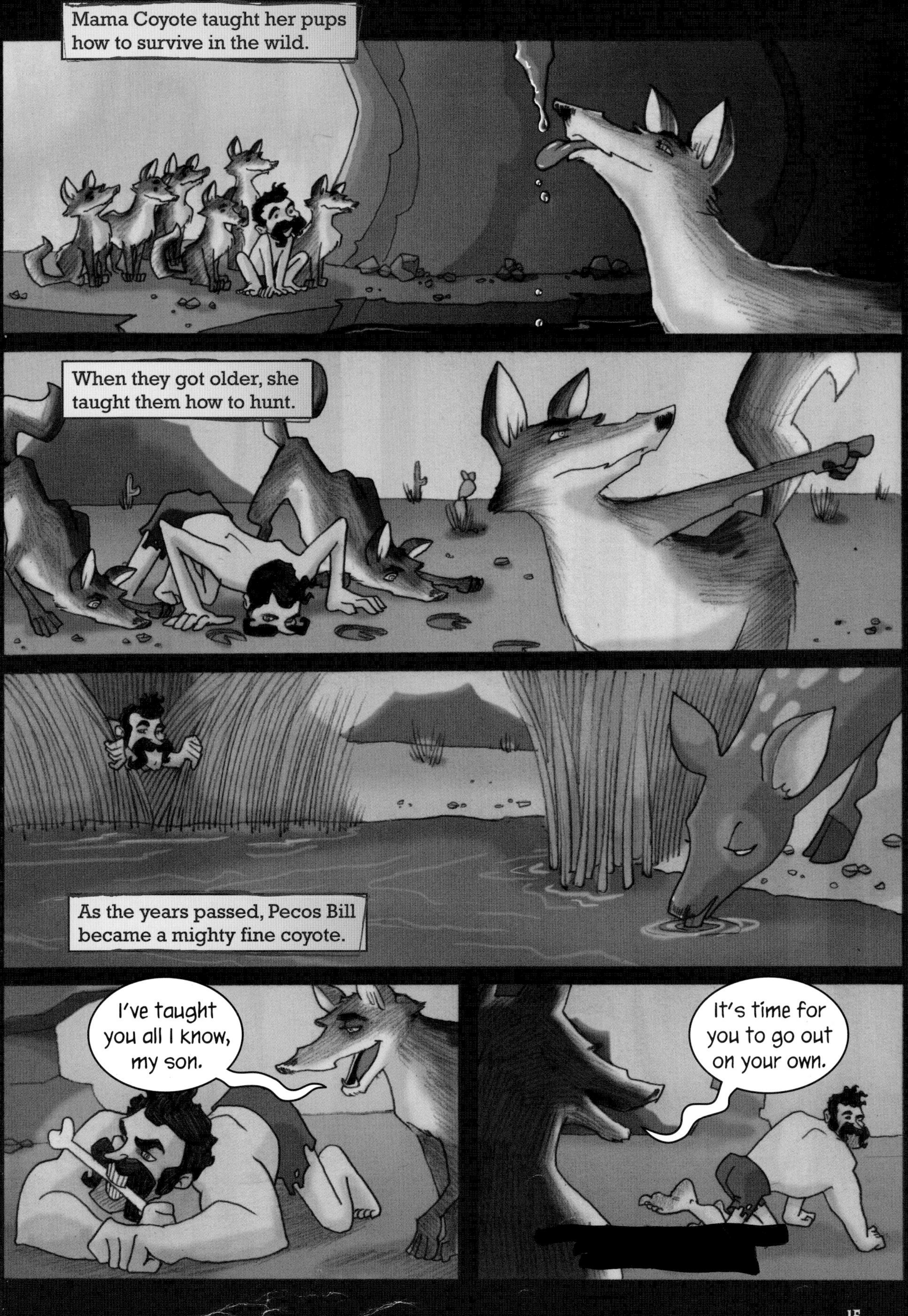
Mama Coyote taught her pups how to survive in the wild.
When they got older, she taught them how to hunt.
As the years passed, Pecos Bill became a mighty fine coyote.
I've taught you all I know, my son.
It's time for you to go out on your own.

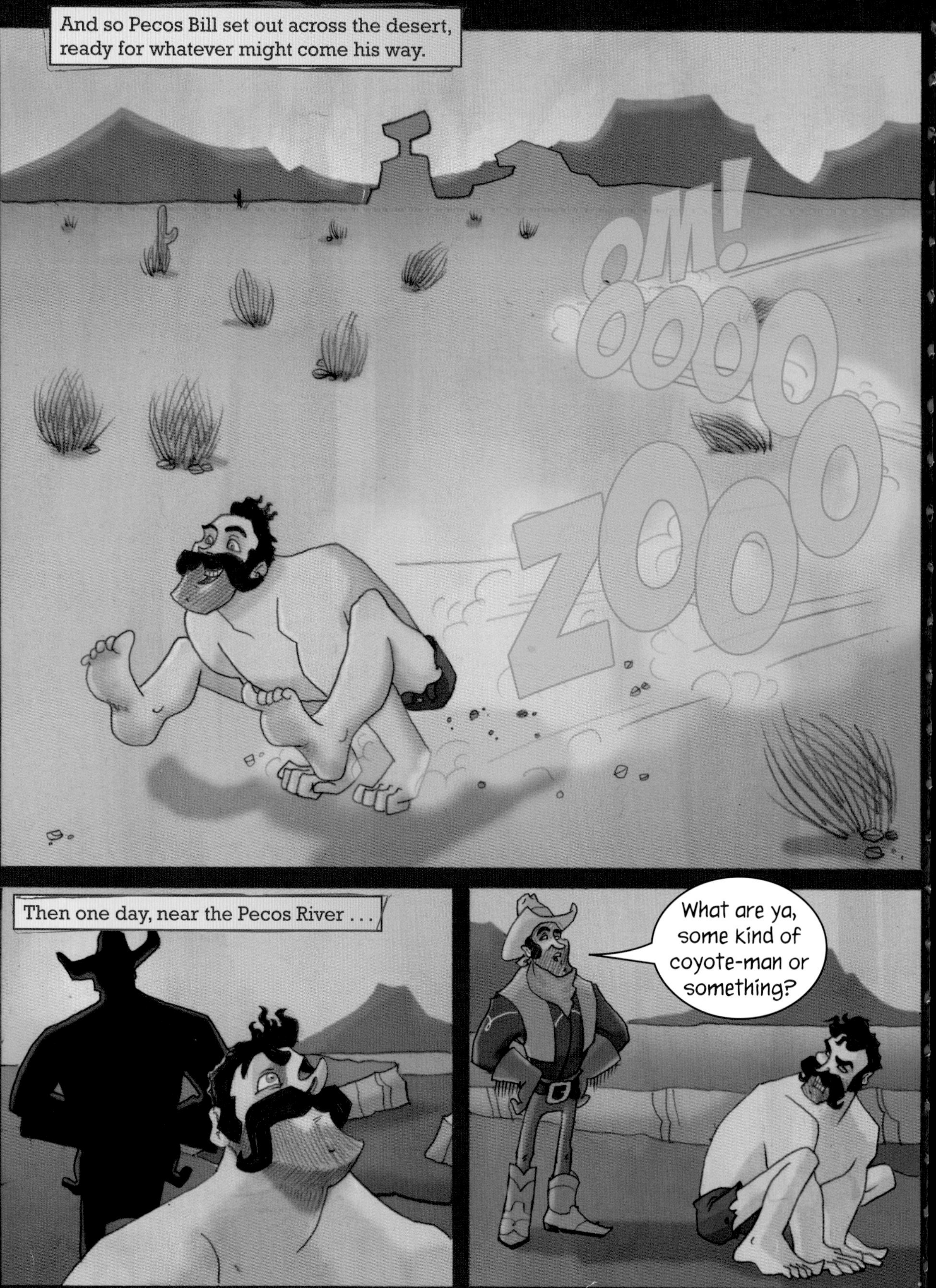
And so Pecos Bill set out across the desert, ready for whatever might come his way.
ZOOOOOOOOM!
Then one day, near the Pecos River . . .
What are ya, some kind of coyote-man or something?

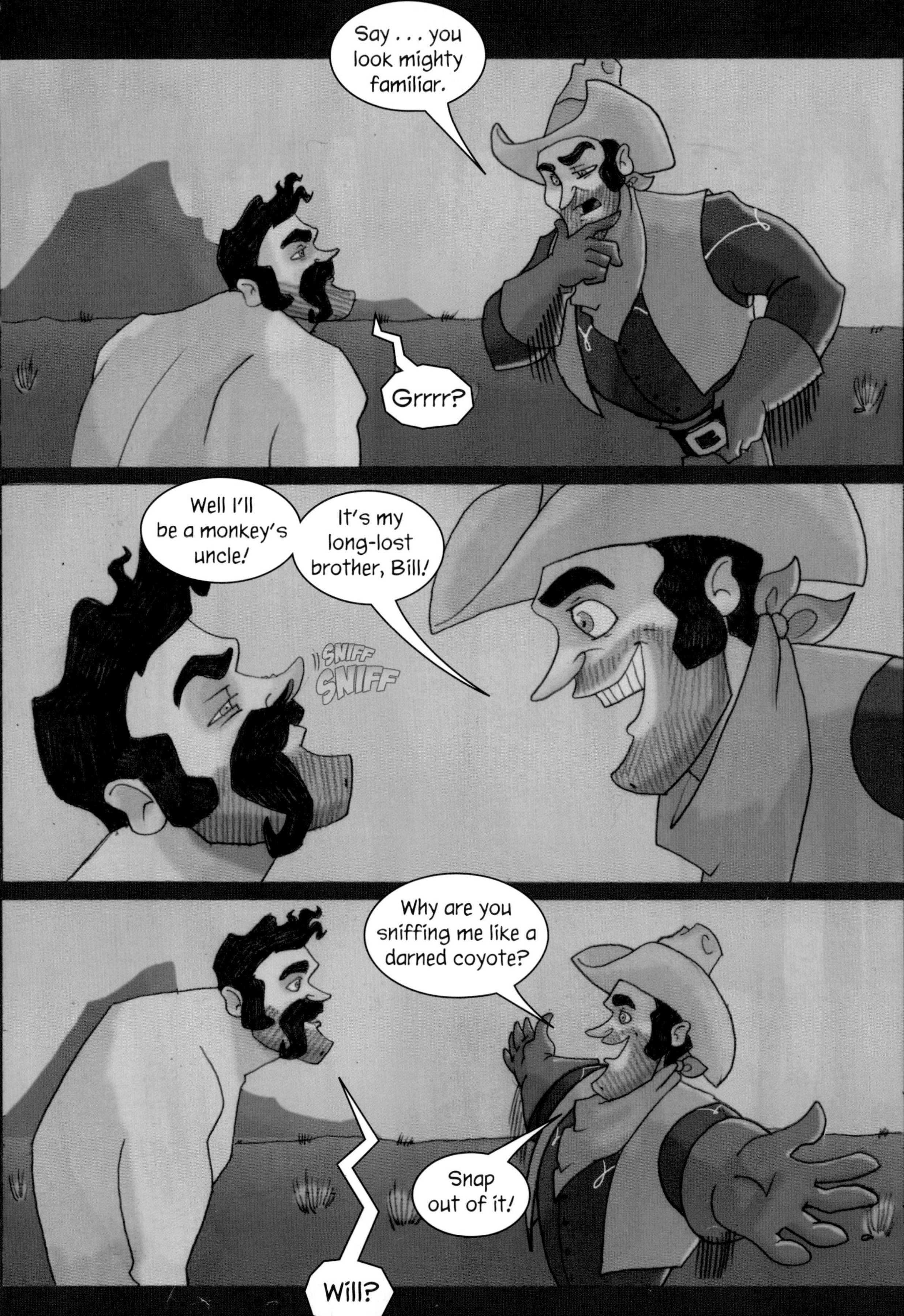
Say . . . you look mighty familiar.
Grrrr?
Well I'll be a monkey's uncle!
It's my long-lost brother, Bill!
SNIFF SNIFF
Why are you sniffing me like a darned coyote?
Snap out of it!
Will?

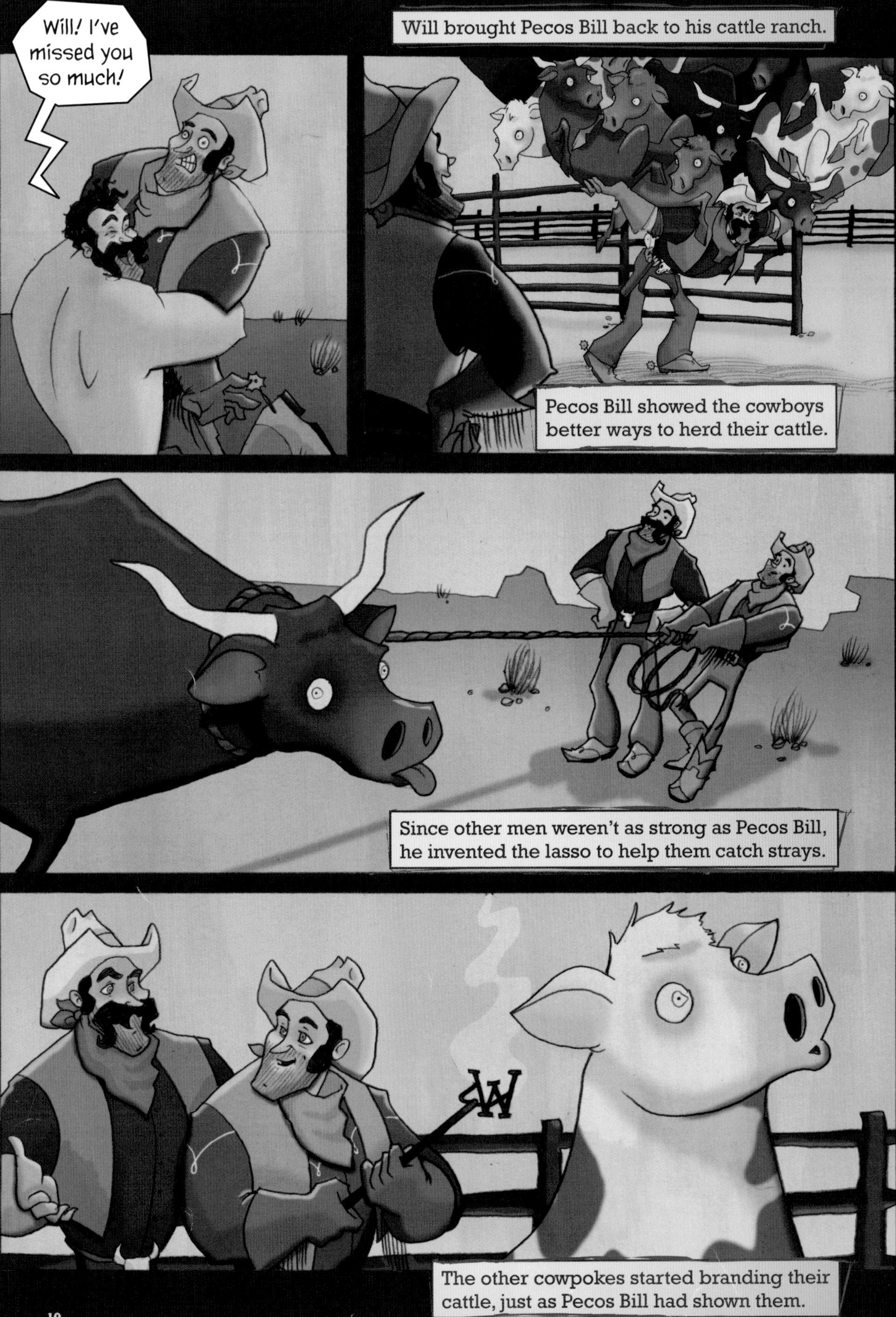
Will brought Pecos Bill back to his cattle ranch.
Will! I've missed you so much!
Pecos Bill showed the cowboys better ways to herd their cattle.
Since other men weren't as strong as Pecos Bill, he invented the lasso to help them catch strays.
The other cowpokes started branding their cattle, just as Pecos Bill had shown them.

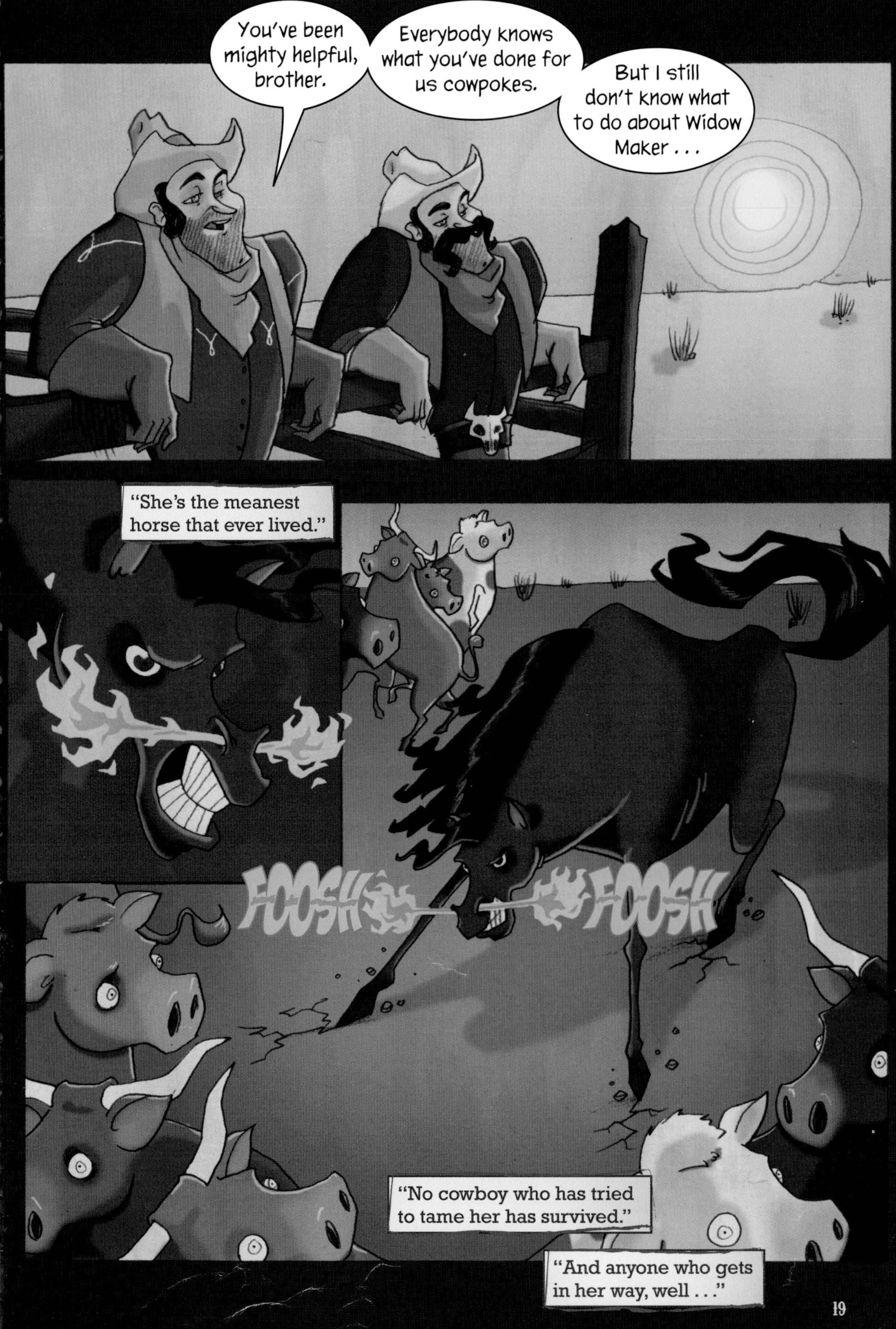
You've been mighty helpful, brother.
Everybody knows what you've done for us cowpokes.
But I still don't know what to do about Widow Maker . . .
"She's the meanest horse that ever lived."
FOOSH
FOOSH
"No cowboy who has tried to tame her has survived."
"And anyone who gets in her way, well . . ."

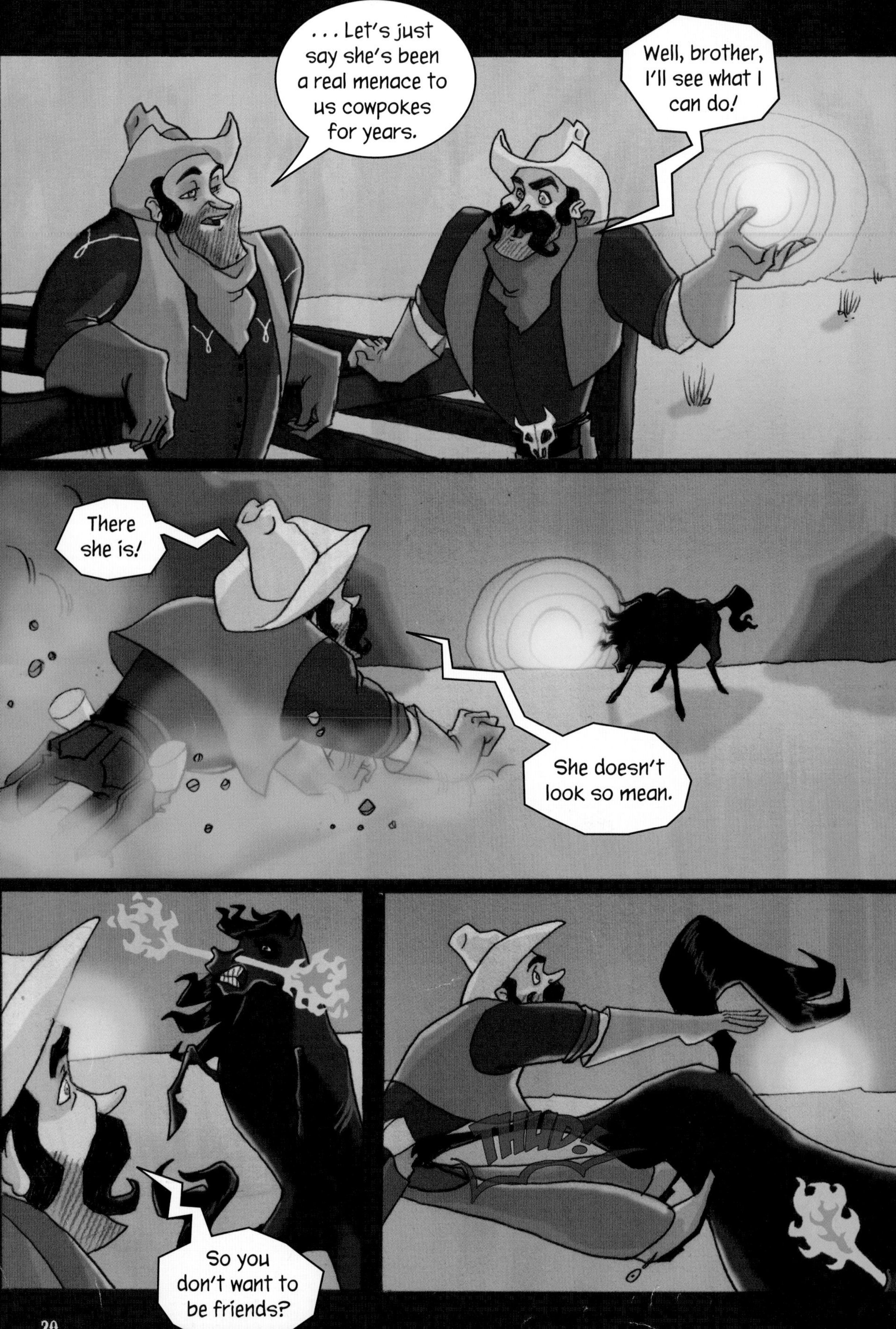
. . . Let's just say she's been a real menace to us cowpokes for years.
Well, brother, I'll see what I can do!
There she is!
She doesn't look so mean.
So you don't want to be friends?
THUD!

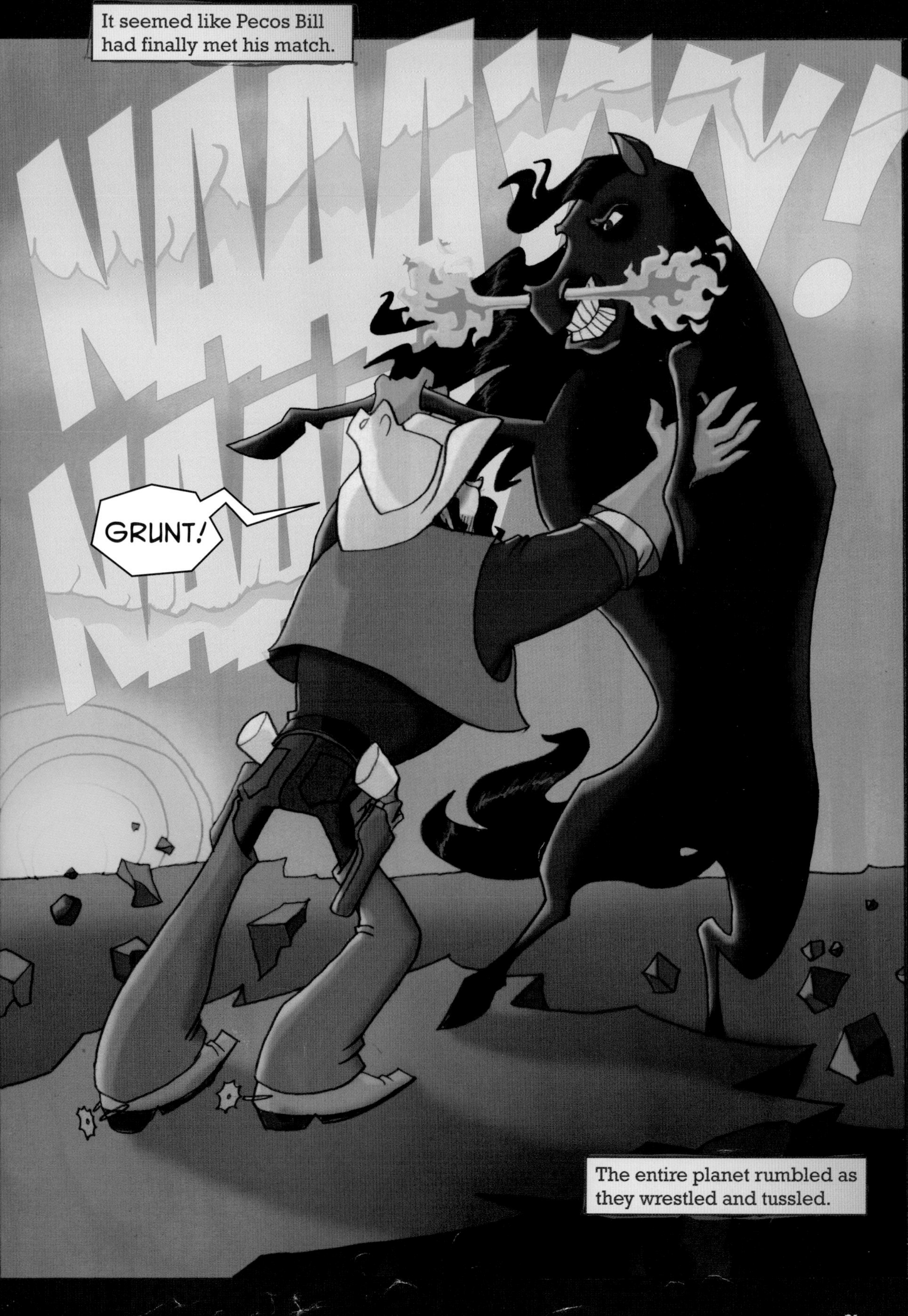
It seemed like Pecos Bill had finally met his match.
GRUNT!
The entire planet rumbled as they wrestled and tussled.

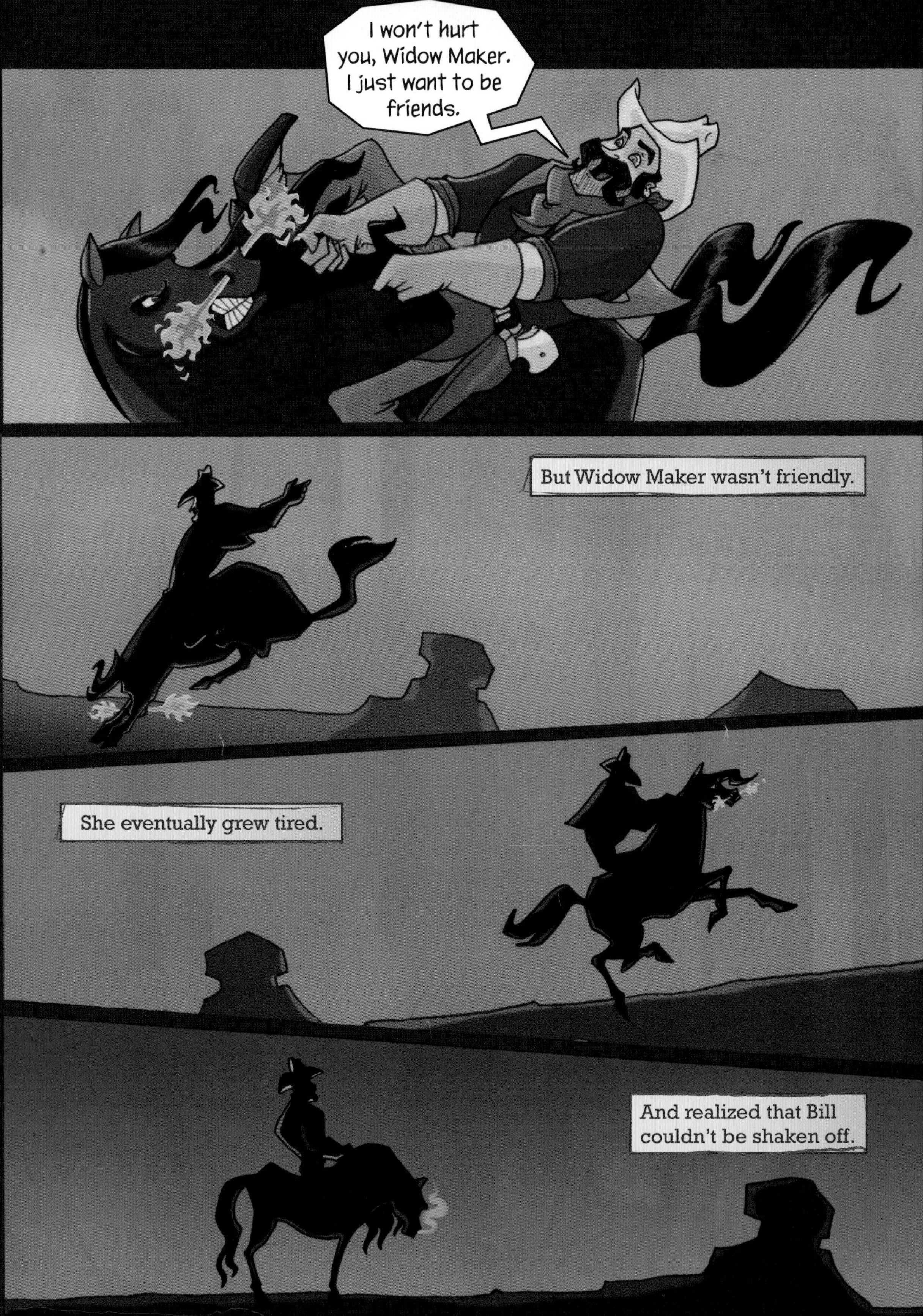
I won't hurt you, Widow Maker. I just want to be friends.
But Widow Maker wasn't friendly.
She eventually grew tired.
And realized that Bill couldn't be shaken off.

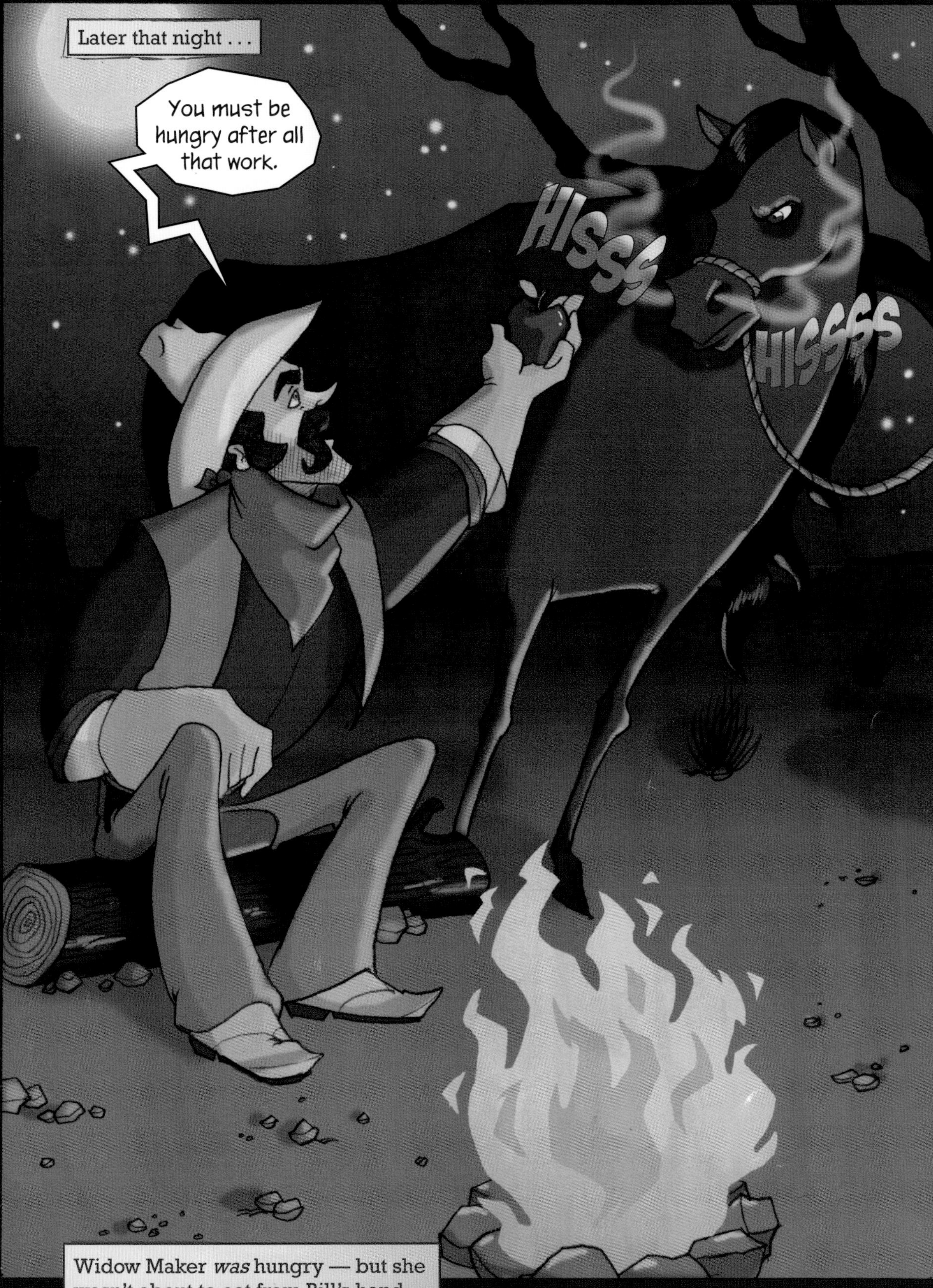

Later that night . . .
You must be hungry after all that work.
HISSS
HISSSS
Widow Maker *was* hungry — but she wasn't about to eat from Bill's hand.

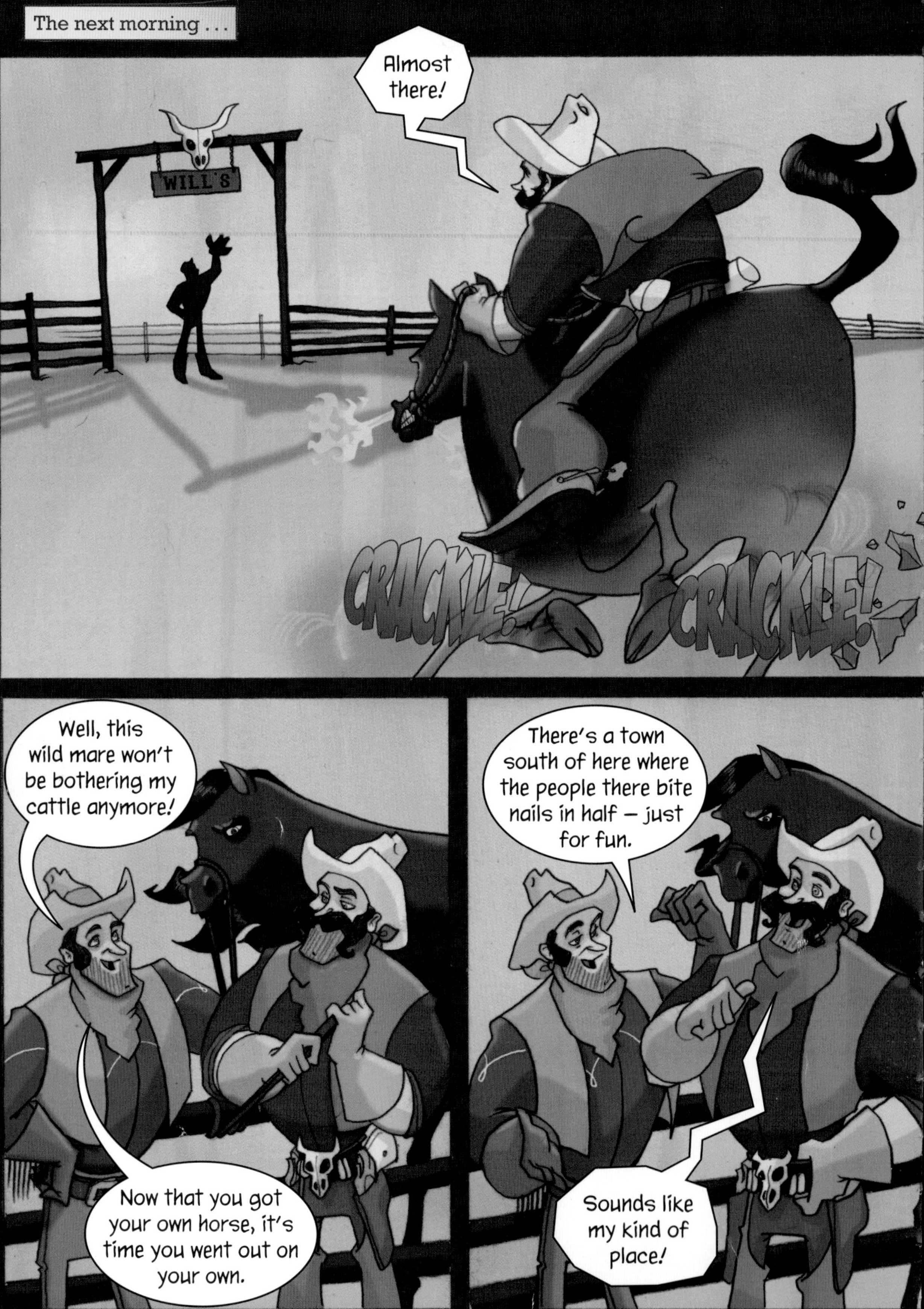
The next morning . . .
Almost there!
WILL'S
CRACKLE! CRACKLE!
Well, this wild mare won't be bothering my cattle anymore!
Now that you got your own horse, it's time you went out on your own.
There's a town south of here where the people there bite nails in half — just for fun.
Sounds like my kind of place!

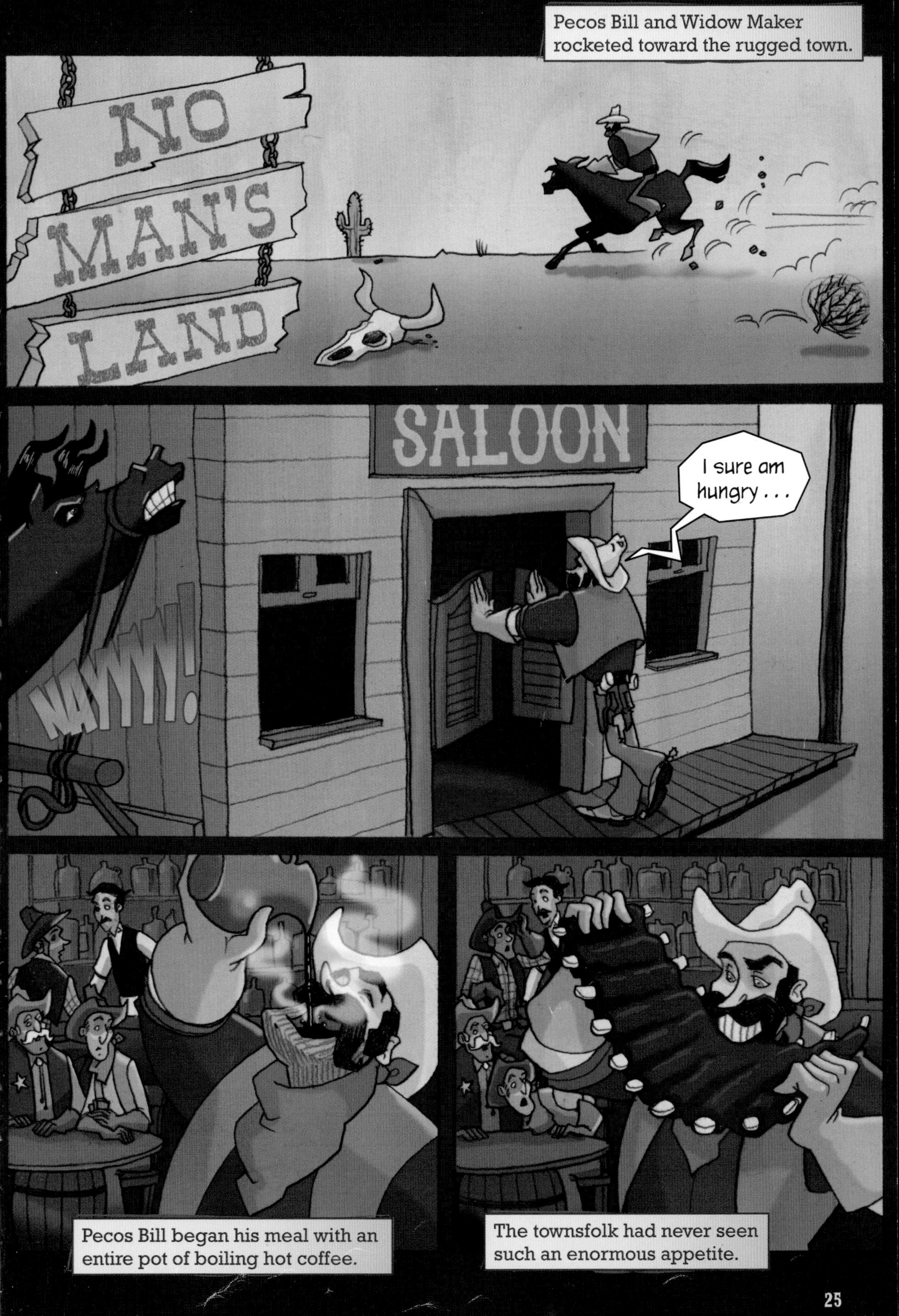
Pecos Bill and Widow Maker rocketed toward the rugged town.
NO MAN'S LAND
SALOON
I sure am hungry . . .
Pecos Bill began his meal with an entire pot of boiling hot coffee.
The townsfolk had never seen such an enormous appetite.

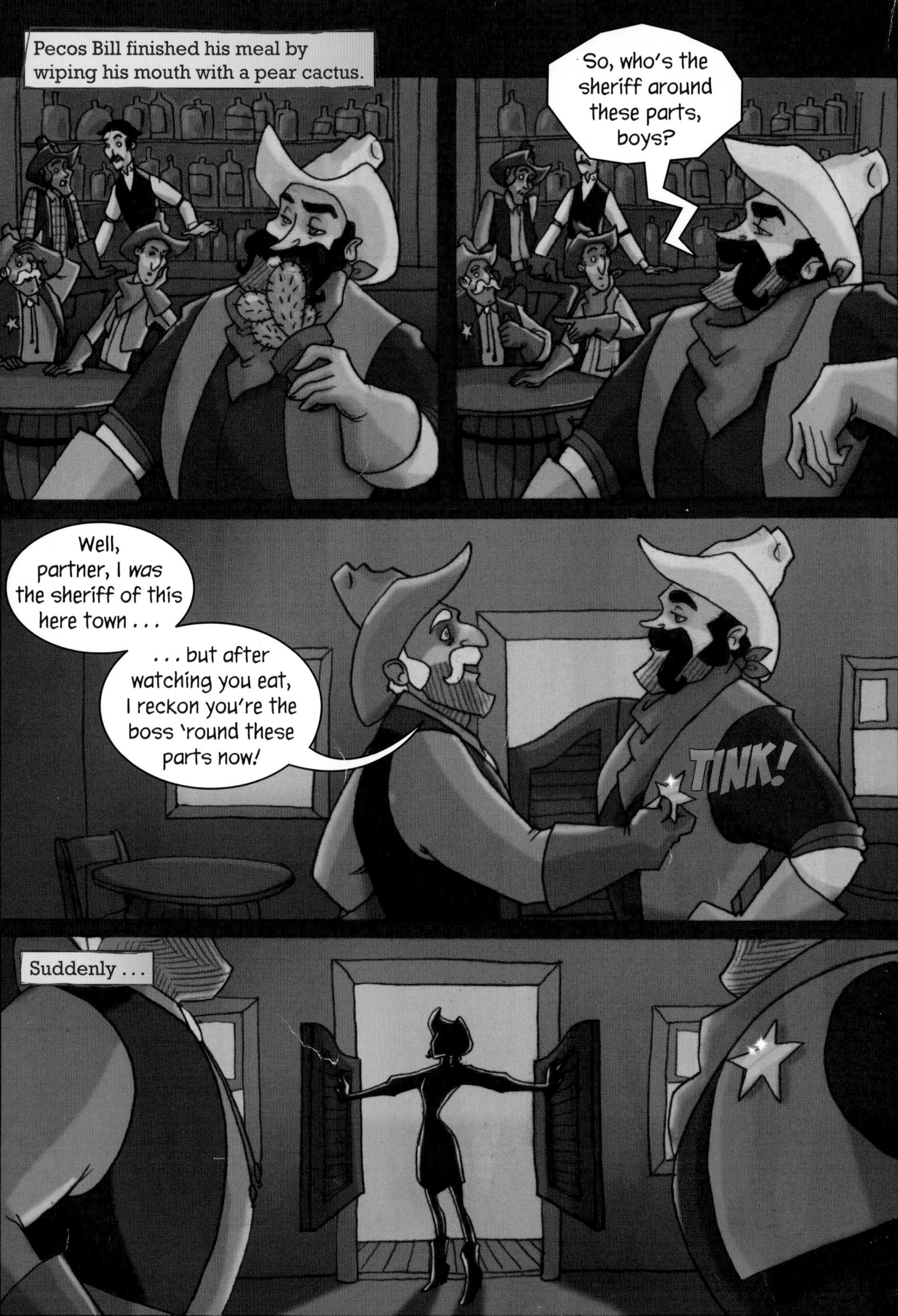

Pecos Bill finished his meal by wiping his mouth with a pear cactus.
So, who's the sheriff around these parts, boys?
Well, partner, I *was* the sheriff of this here town . . .
. . . but after watching you eat, I reckon you're the boss 'round these parts now!
TINK!
Suddenly . . .

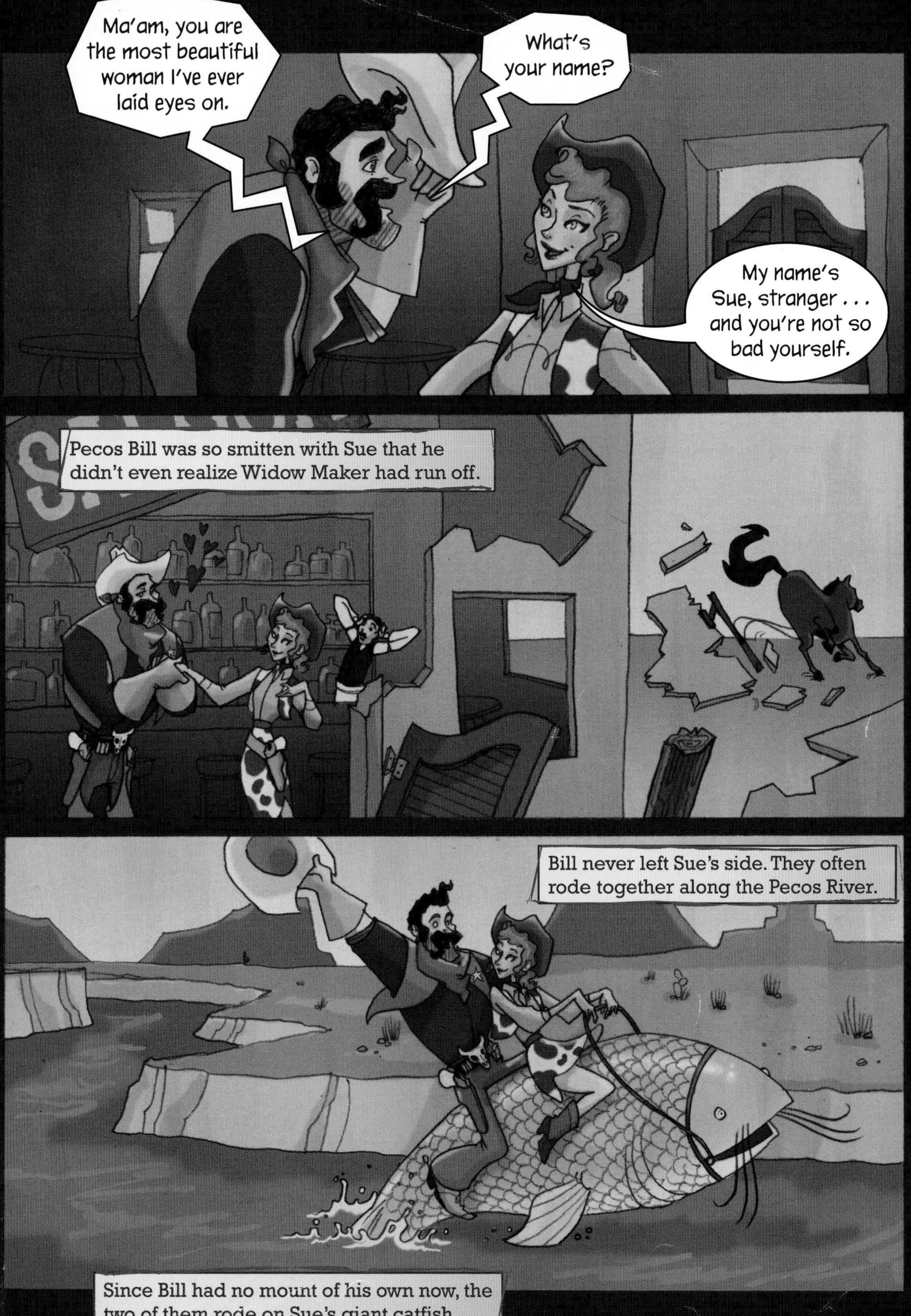

Ma'am, you are the most beautiful woman I've ever laid eyes on.
What's your name?
My name's Sue, stranger . . . and you're not so bad yourself.
Pecos Bill was so smitten with Sue that he didn't even realize Widow Maker had run off.
Bill never left Sue's side. They often rode together along the Pecos River.
Since Bill had no mount of his own now, the two of them rode on Sue's giant catfish.

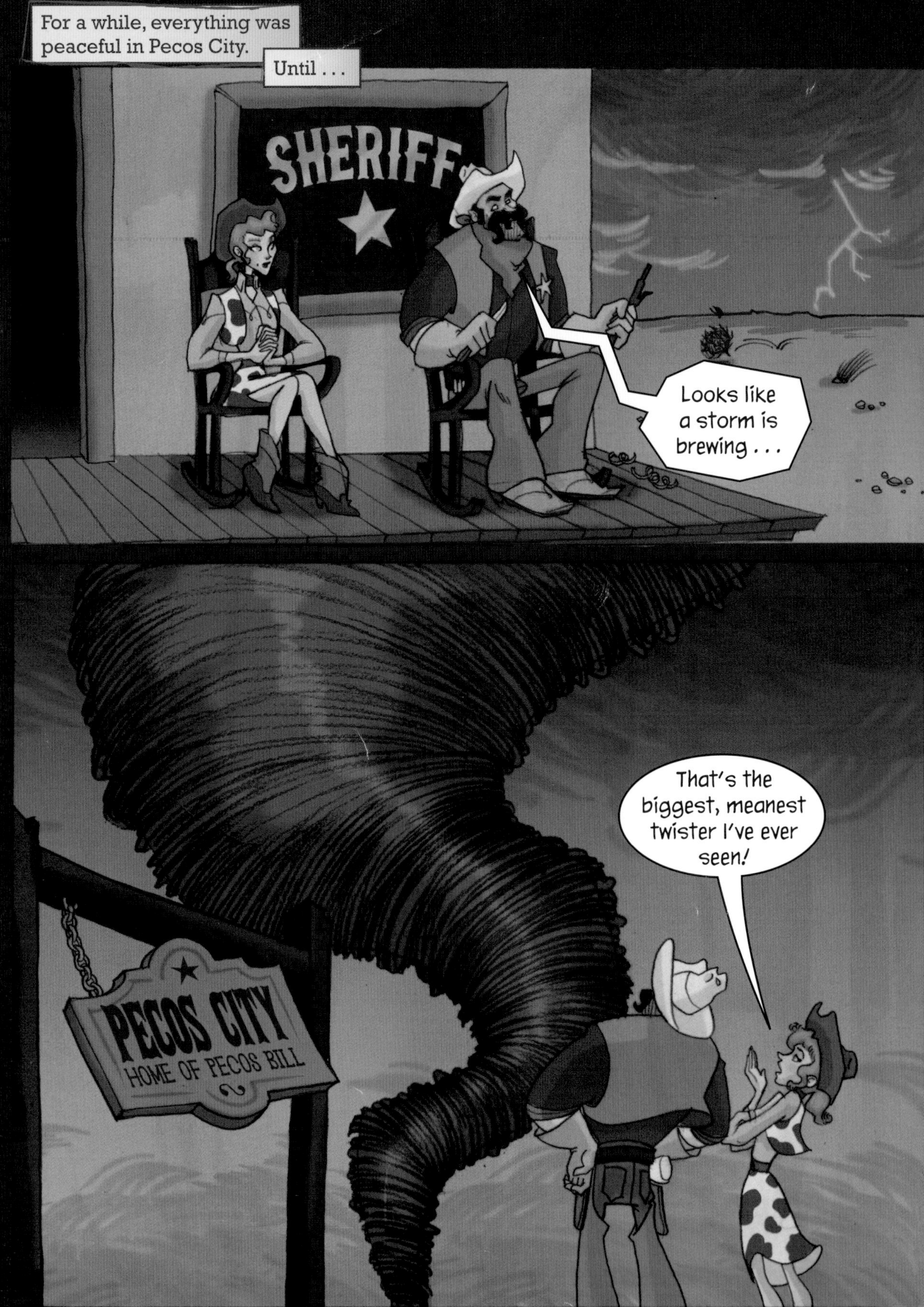
For a while, everything was peaceful in Pecos City.
Until . . .
SHERIFF
Looks like a storm is brewing . . .
That's the biggest, meanest twister I've ever seen!
PECOS CITY
HOME OF PECOS BILL

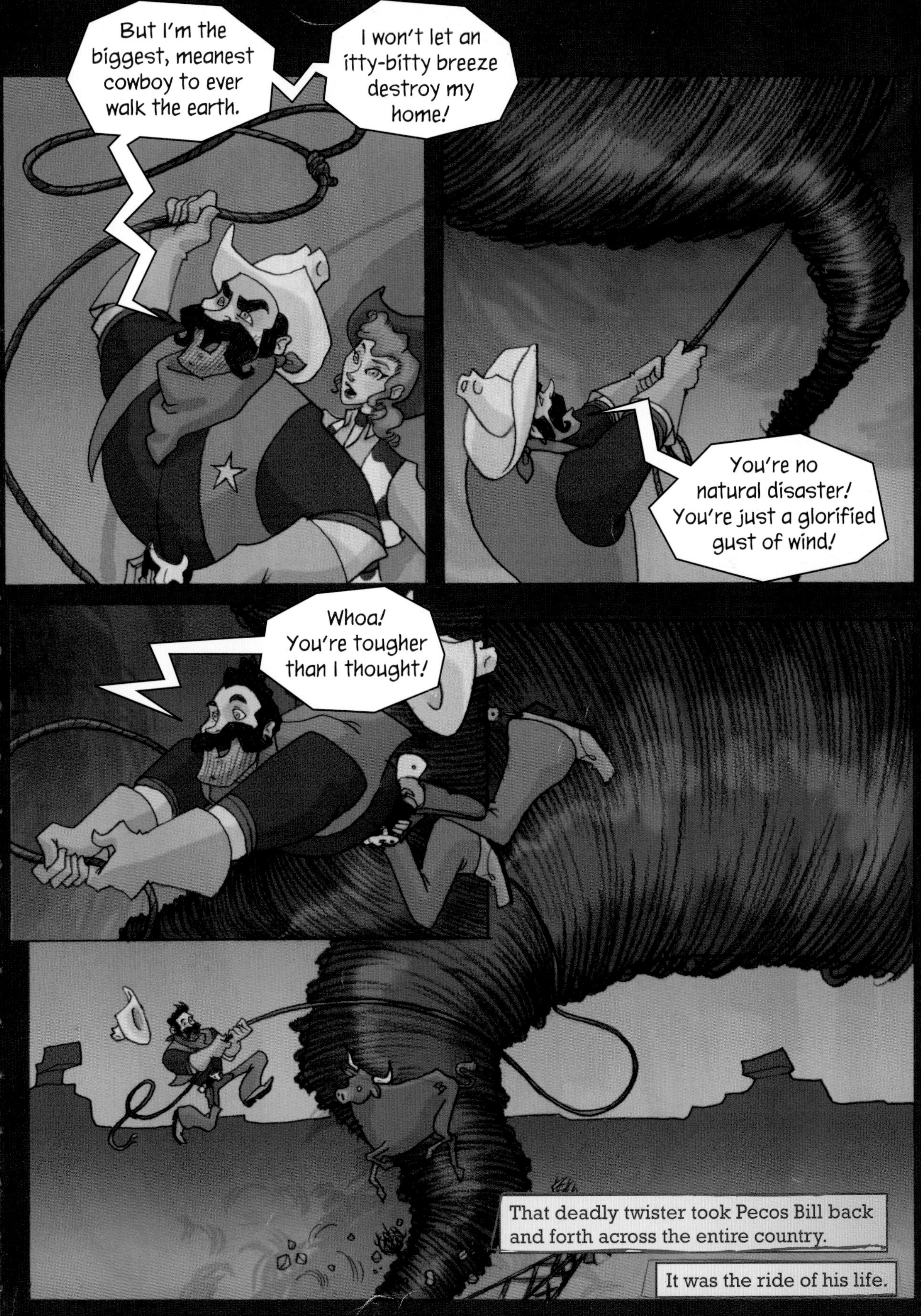

But I'm the biggest, meanest cowboy to ever walk the earth.
I won't let an itty-bitty breeze destroy my home!
You're no natural disaster! You're just a glorified gust of wind!
Whoa! You're tougher than I thought!
That deadly twister took Pecos Bill back and forth across the entire country.
It was the ride of his life.

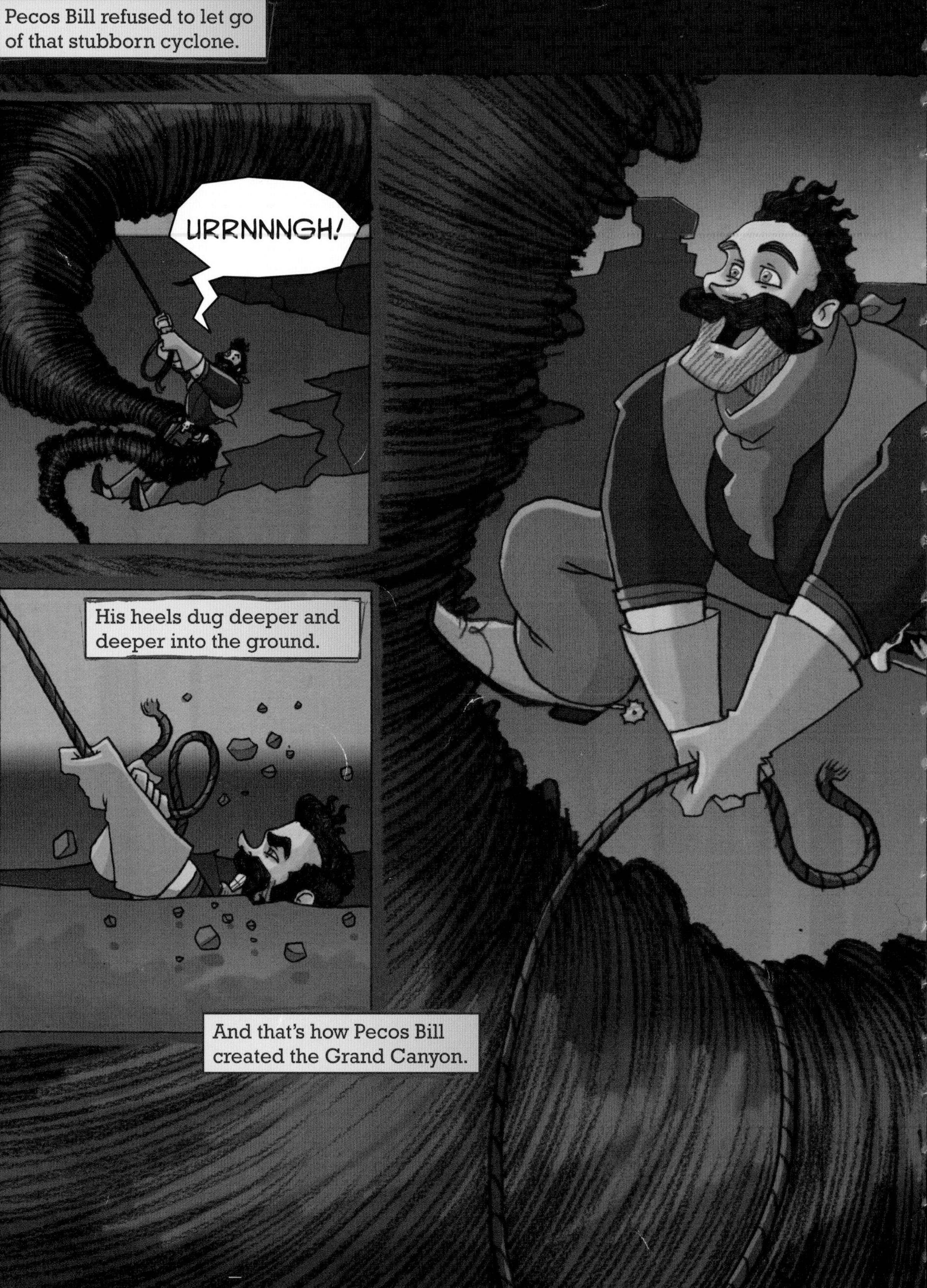
Pecos Bill refused to let go of that stubborn cyclone.
URRNNNGH!
His heels dug deeper and deeper into the ground.
And that's how Pecos Bill created the Grand Canyon.

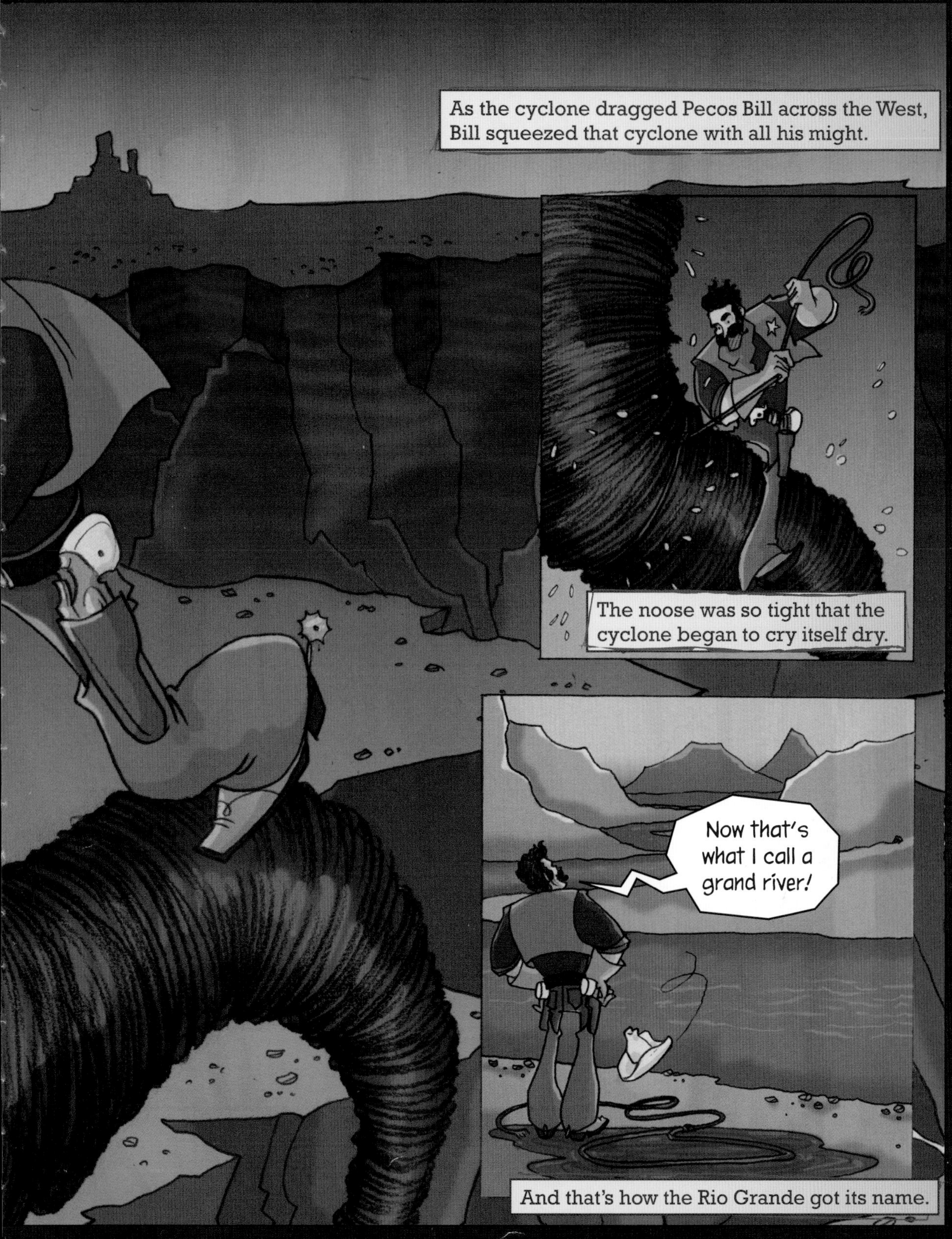
As the cyclone dragged Pecos Bill across the West, Bill squeezed that cyclone with all his might.
The noose was so tight that the cyclone began to cry itself dry.
Now that's what I call a grand river!
And that's how the Rio Grande got its name.

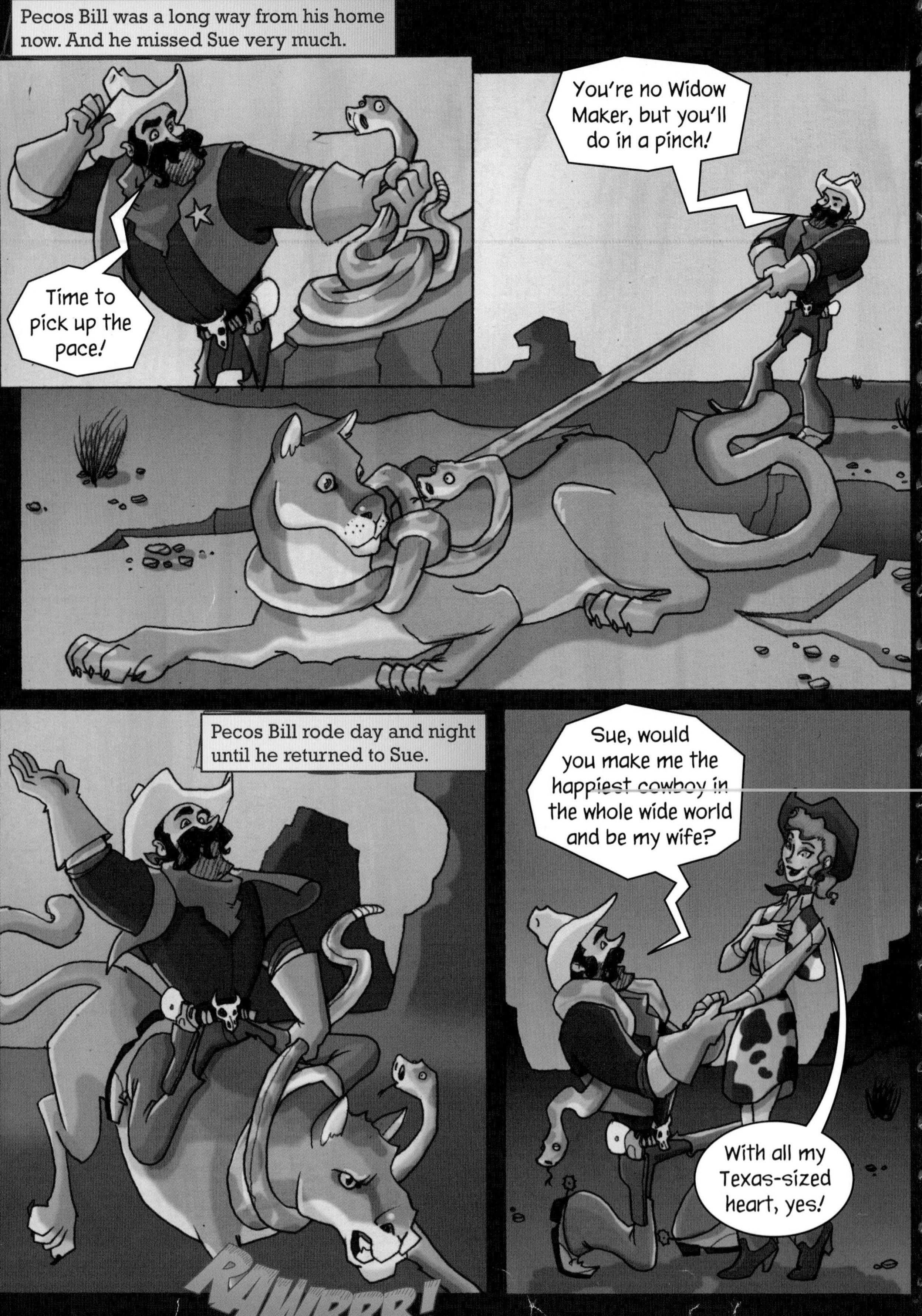

Pecos Bill was a long way from his home now. And he missed Sue very much.
Time to pick up the pace!
You're no Widow Maker, but you'll do in a pinch!
Pecos Bill rode day and night until he returned to Sue.
RAWRRR!
Sue, would you make me the happiest cowboy in the whole wide world and be my wife?
With all my Texas-sized heart, yes!

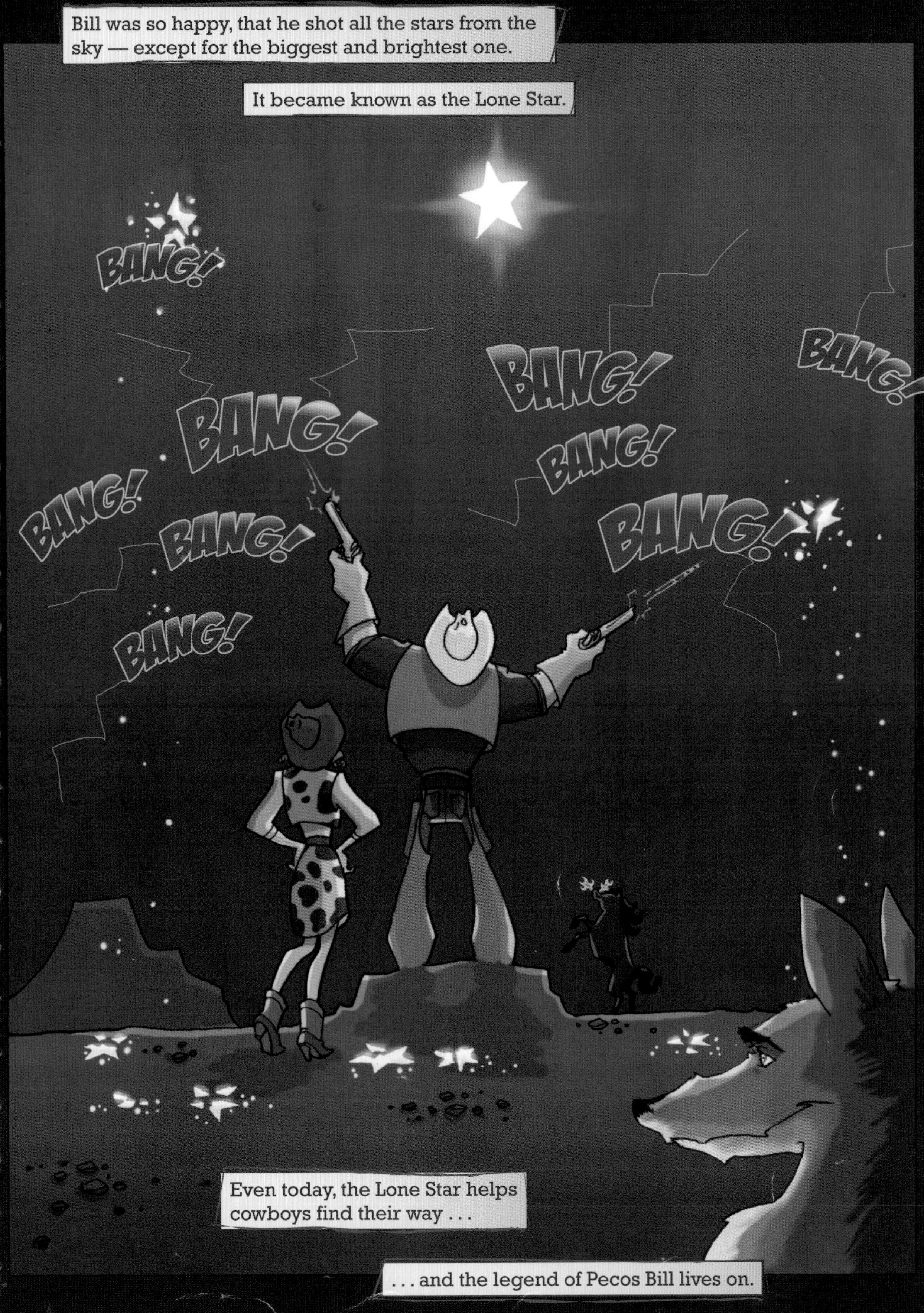
Bill was so happy, that he shot all the stars from the sky — except for the biggest and brightest one.
It became known as the Lone Star.
BANG!
BANG!
BANG!
BANG!
BANG!
BANG!
BANG!
BANG!
BANG!
Even today, the Lone Star helps cowboys find their way . . .
. . . and the legend of Pecos Bill lives on.

# ABOUT THE AUTHOR

## SEAN TULIEN

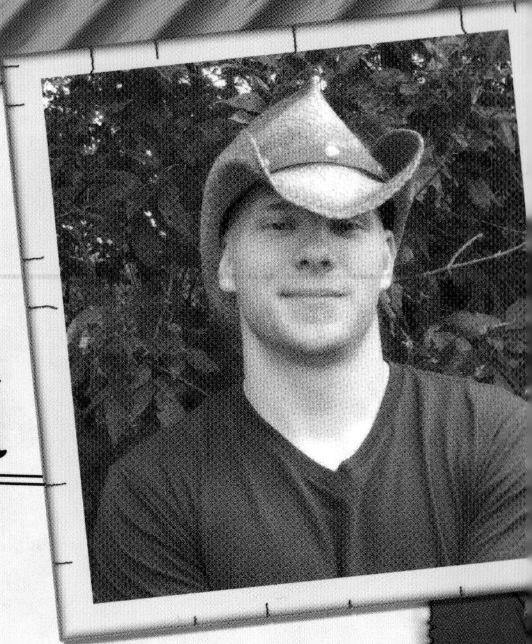

Sean Tulien is a children's book editor living and working in Minnesota. In his spare time, he likes to read, eat sushi, exercise outdoors, listen to loud music, and write books like this one. Sean has loved the legend of Pecos Bill ever since he was a little cowpoke, so turning the tall tale into a graphic novel was a big thrill for him. Sean also thinks cows are really funny, and his favorite animals are manatees, wolves, and eels.

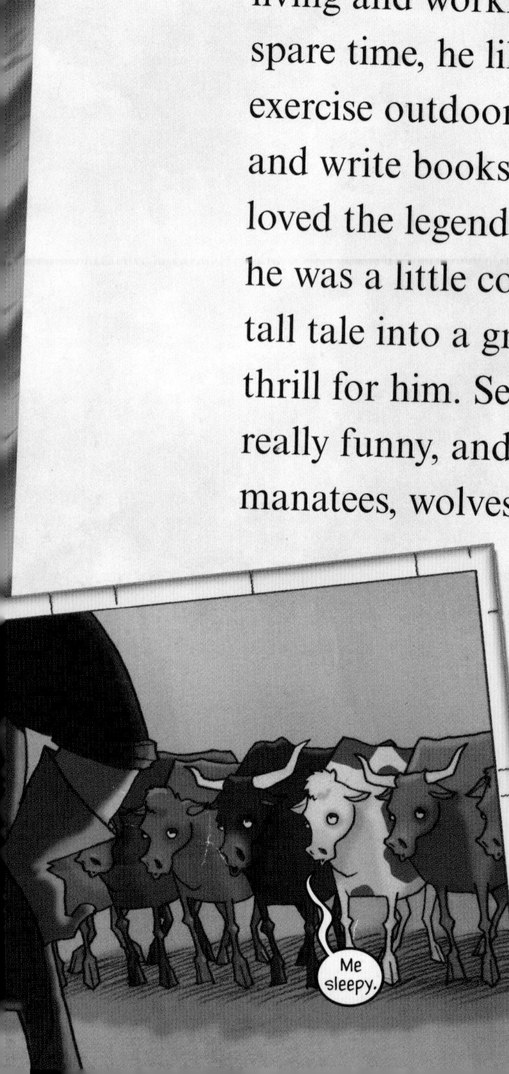
Me sleepy.

CONFIDENTIAL INFORMATION
WILD WEST TRIBUNE

# ABOUT THE ILLUSTRATOR

## LISA K. WEBER

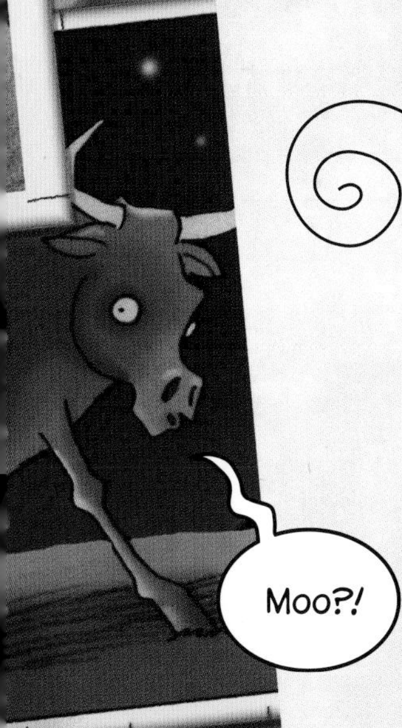
Moo?!

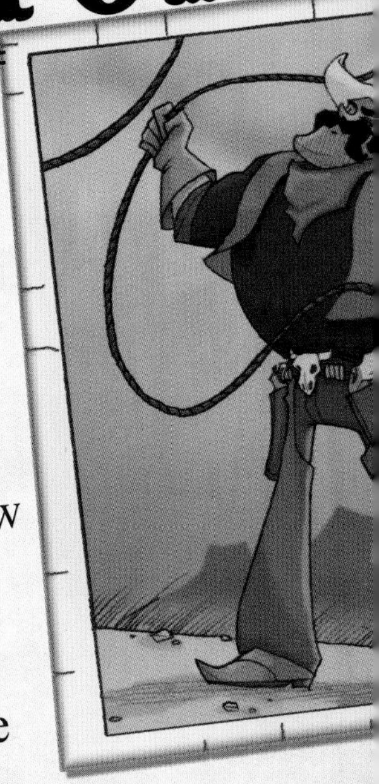

Lisa K. Weber is an artist who lives and works in Oakland, California. She graduated from Parsons School of Design in New York with a BFA in Illustration in 2000. Her whimsically quirky characters and illustrations have appeared in various print and animation projects for Scholastic, Graphic Classics, Children's Television Workshop, and many others.

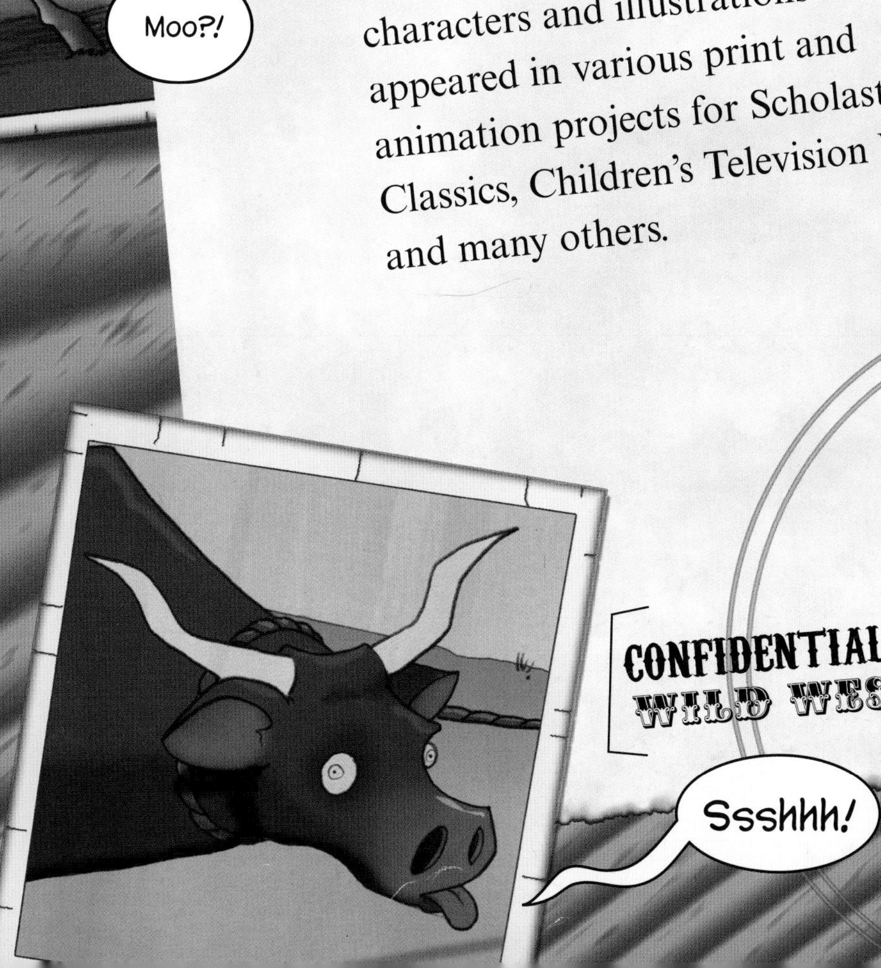
Ssshhh!

CONFIDENTIAL INFORMATION
WILD WEST TRIBUNE

# WILD WEST

**Vol. 49   No. 26**     **SAN ANTONIO, TEXAS U.S.A**

# THE LEGEND OF PECOS BILL

## Folklore or "Fakelore"?

Some historians believe the tall tales of Pecos Bill were invented by settlers of the American Southwest during the early 1800s. Others believe the stories came much later. In 1916, author Edward O'Reilly first published the tales in *The Century Magazine.* Later, he reprinted them in a book titled *Saga of Pecos Bill.* O'Reilly claimed that the book was a collection of cowboy folklore, or stories passed down from generation to generation. Today, however, most experts believe that O'Reilly made the stories up. Either way, Pecos Bill remains an American legend.

## THE TALL TALE OF AMERICA'S GREATEST COWBOY CONTINUES

Dozens of comics, children's books, and cartoons have featured Pecos Bill. Author James Cloyd Bowman wrote *Pecos Bill: The Greatest Cowboy of All Time,* perhaps the most famous collection of tall tales about the American legend. In 1938, the book won a Newbery Award, which is one of the highest honors in children's literature. Ten years later, the Walt Disney Company released an animated movie featuring the colossal cowboy.

## COWBOY CARVES CANYON WITH HIS BOOTS

Legend states that Pecos Bill created the Grand Canyon by lassoing a cyclone. However, scientists believe the 277-mile-long gulch, which runs through Arizona, was formed by erosion. For three to six million years, the Colorado River wore down the desert rock. Today, the canyon depth averages more than one mile.

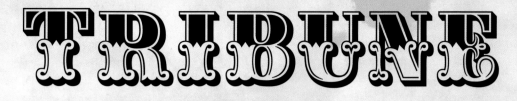

# TRIBUNE

* SPECIAL COMMEMORATIVE EDITION * April 1

## MOON OR HONEYMOON?

Pecos Bill's hopes for a Wild West honeymoon with his bride-to-be, Slue-Foot Sue, were dashed when Sue attempted to ride Widow Maker. Details are unclear, but it appears that Sue was bucked so high into the sky that she struck her head on the moon. Her bustle (a spring-loaded piece of clothing) sent her bouncing back and forth between the Moon and Earth. The bouncing continued for several days, until Pecos Bill snared Sue with his rattlesnake lasso. Unhurt, but shaken, Sue swore off cowboys — including Pecos Bill — for the rest of her life.

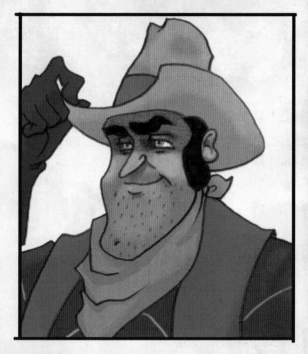

## THE DEADLY DEBATE

Pecos Bill's greatness is undeniable, but his death is the cause of some debate. Many tales state that a diet of fishhooks and nitroglycerin, a poisonous liquid, finally killed the colossal cowboy. Others say that Pecos died laughing at foolish Texas tourists, who dressed in ten-gallon hats and called themselves cowboys. Like the legend of Pecos Bill, this debate may live on forever.

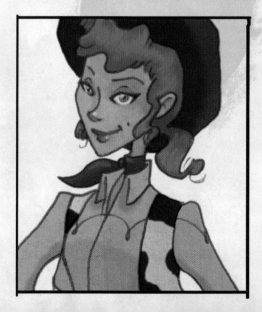

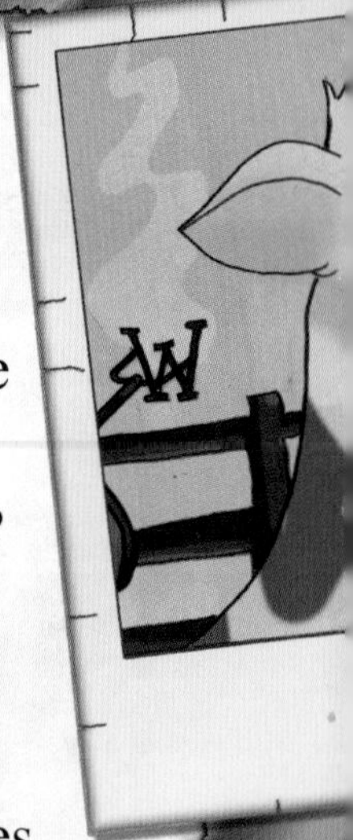

# Discussion Questions

1. Many famous sites appear in this book, including the Grand Canyon and the Rio Grande. Have you ever visited these places? What are some sites you've seen?
2. The tall tale of Pecos Bill has a lot of exaggeration, but what parts of this story could have been real?
3. Pecos Bill meets many interesting people and creatures in his adventures. Who was your favorite? Why?

# Writing Prompts

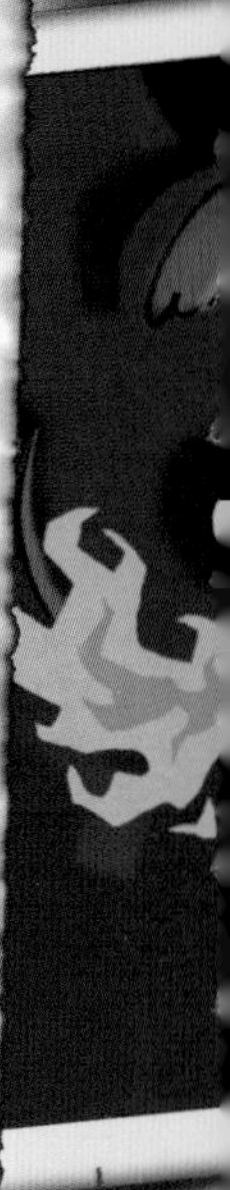

1. At the ending of this book, Pecos Bill and Sue decide to get married. What kinds of crazy adventures will they have together? Write about it.
2. Tall tales are often made-up stories about how amazing things were created. Pecos Bill, for example, created the Grand Canyon when he was riding a cyclone. Think of some amazing things on Earth, and make up explanations about how they were created.
3. Pecos Bill rides a coyote, a wild mare, and a mountain lion in this book. If you could have any type of creature to ride, what kind of animal would it be? Write about your new mount. Then draw a picture of it.

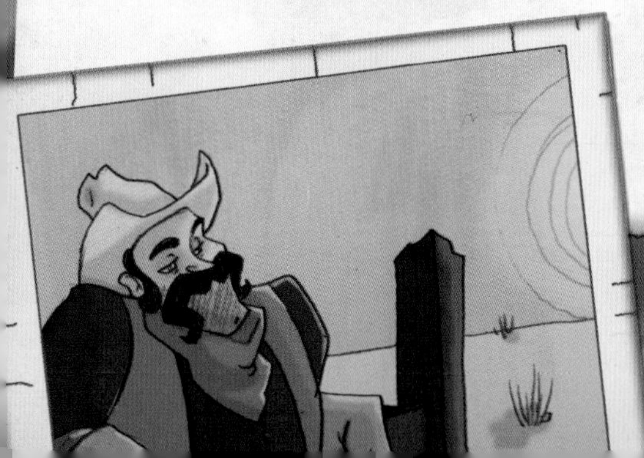

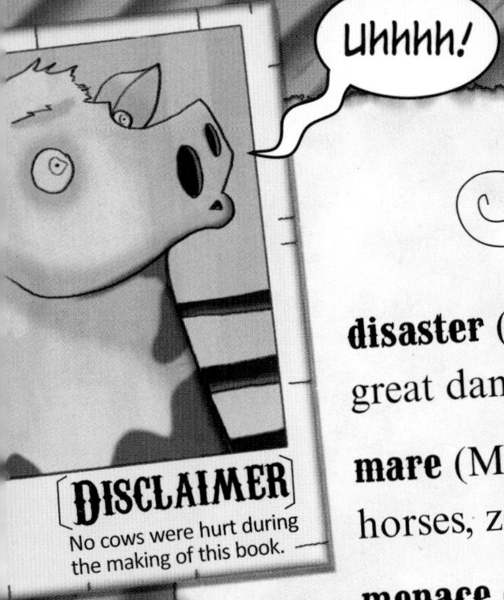
Uhhhh!
DISCLAIMER
No cows were hurt during the making of this book.

# GLOSSARY

**disaster** (duh-ZASS-tur)—an event that causes great damage, loss, or suffering

**mare** (MAIR)—the female of certain animals like horses, zebras, and donkeys

**menace** (MEN-iss)—a threat or danger

**obedient** (oh-BEE-dee-uhnt)—if you are obedient, you do what you are told to do

**ranch** (RANCH)—a large farm for cattle, sheep, or horses

**reckon** (REK-uhn)—to think or have an opinion

**smitten** (SMIH-tehn)—deeply affected by something

**stray** (STRAY)—a lost animal that wanders away from the herd

**stubborn** (STUHB-urn)—not willing to change, or set on having your own way

**tussled** (TUHSS-uhld)—fought or struggled vigorously

**utter** (UHT-ur)—complete or total

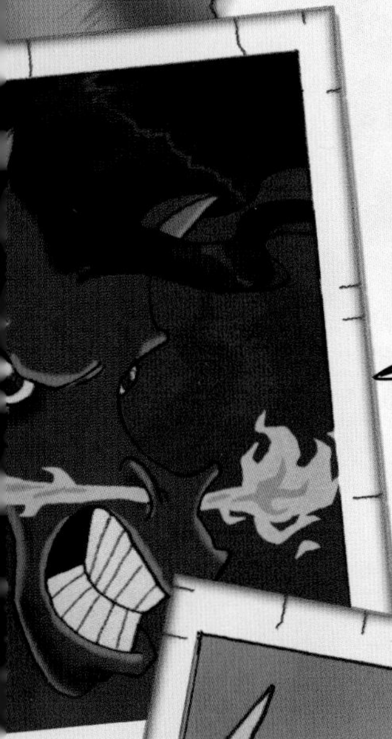

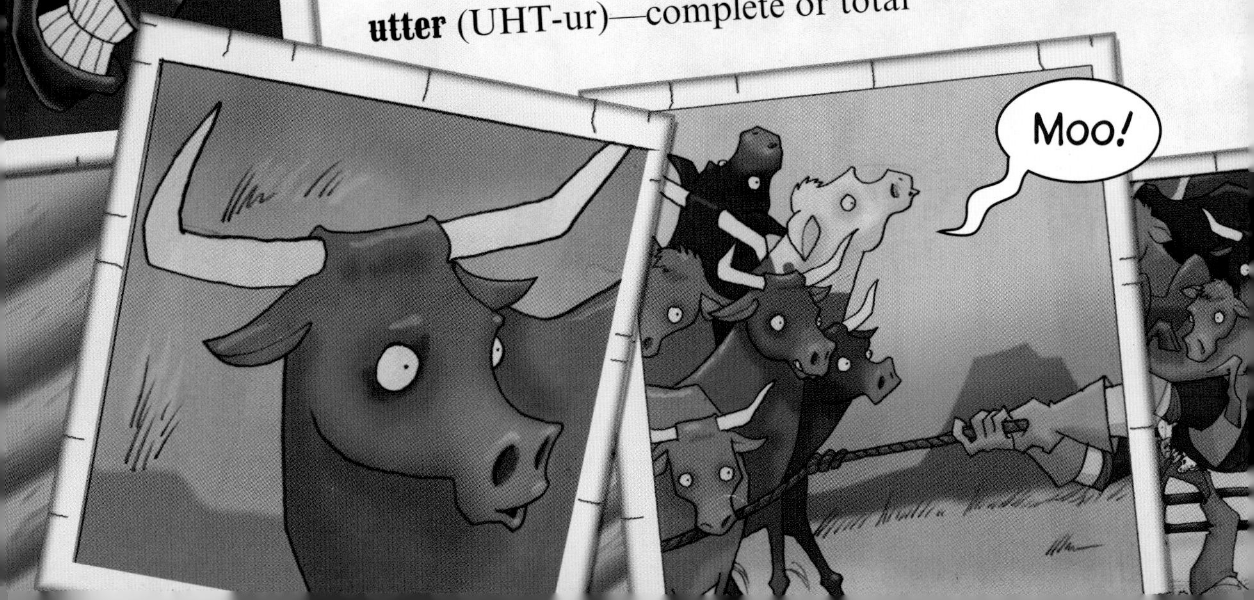
Moo!

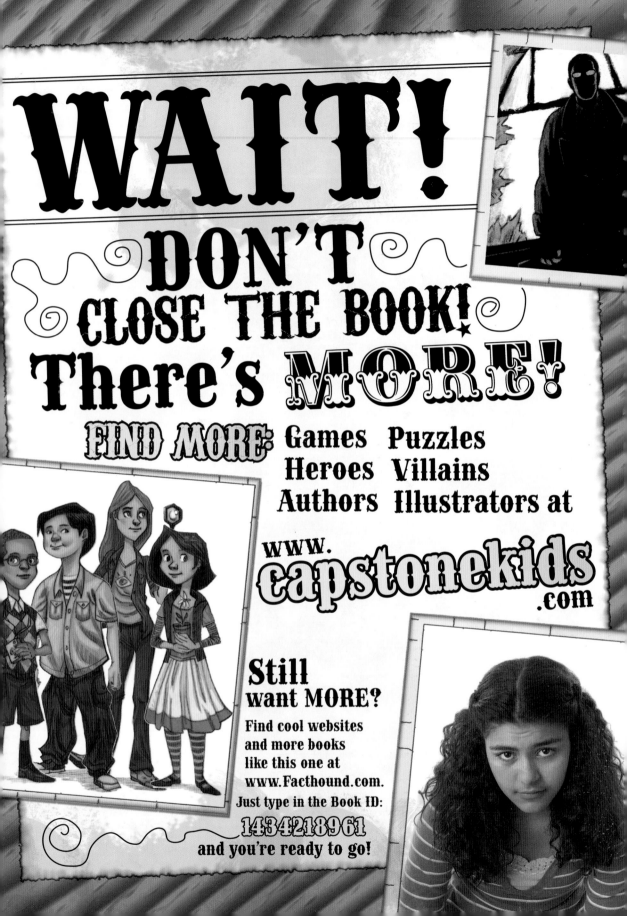

[redacted]